MW01031572

LIVE UNITED

United Way
of Portage County
www.uwportage.org

ALSO BY GRACE CHETWIN

Child of the Air
Collidescope
On All Hallow's Eve
Out of the Dark World
Friends in Time

Tales of Gom
Gom on Windy Mountain
The Riddle and the Rune
The Crystal Stair
The Starstone

GRACE CHETWIN

The Chimes of Alyafaleyn

BRADBURY PRESS New York

Maxwell Macmillan Canada   Toronto
Maxwell Macmillan International
New York Oxford Singapore Sydney

Copyright ©1993 By Grace Chetwin

All rights reserved. No part of this book may be reproduced or transmitted in any form or by any means, electronic or mechanical, including photocopying, recording, or by any information storage and retrieval system, without permission in writing from the Publisher.

Bradbury Press
Macmillan Publishing Company
866 Third Avenue
New York, NY 10022

Maxwell Macmillan Canada, Inc.
1200 Eglinton Avenue East
Suite 200
Don Mills, Ontario M3C 3N1

Macmillan Publishing Company is part of the Maxwell Communication Group of Companies.

First edition
Printed and bound in the United States of America
10 9 8 7 6 5 4 3 2 1

The text of this book is set in 12-point Meridien.
Typography by Cathy Bobak

Library of Congress Cataloging-in-Publication Data
Chetwin, Grace.
   The chimes of Alyafaleyn / by Grace Chetwin—1st ed.
     p. cm.
   Summary: Into Alyafaleyn, where harmony is kept by the chimes called heynim that people draw to them through the air, are born two special people—Tamborel, who cannot attract heynim, and Caidrun, who has great power over them.
   ISBN 0-02-718222-3
   [1. Fantasy.]   I. Title
PZ7.C42555Ck 1993
[Fic]—dc20   92-44156

For June Alexandra
With Love
Notwithstanding

Part One

•1•

Tamborel slid aside the saba lattice and edged out. From under the shadow of that low stone entrance arch he eyed the knot of women by the garden gate. Eleyna was no gossip, yet there she'd stood all morning, barring his flight with the older boys over the ripening grainfields and on to glory at the minnow brook. Something was up, and it was bad, Tamborel just knew it. Else why did his mother look so grim and why was her back so straight? And why was he kept inside on such a fine day? Had he done something wrong? Tamborel rehearsed all that had been said and done that morning, from the moment he got up to the time Hwyllum, his pappa, left for the grain-

3

fields. And then on till he was sent to wash his face. No, Eleyna had seemed happy with him. So what was it, then? Tamborel raked his fingers through his tawny curls, thinking hard. As he was at the wash-bowl, someone had called Eleyna to the saba lattice. He remembered now the hurried, hushed exchange, and yes, *that* was when she'd told him to stay put.

He inched his bare feet forward until the sunlight on the worn stone step dubbed his big toenail. Still his mother did not turn her head. To have gotten so far undetected! There was no doubting now the dire-ness of the occasion. The women were gazing up the street toward the village boundary, where the road began that led west to Pridicum, the neighboring vil-lage. Were they expecting someone? Tamborel craned on tiptoe, but he was way too small to see over the garden wall.

Above each woman, the modest clusters of their heynim, tiny golden chiming spheres, danced and swirled like sun-bugs with each nod and shake of the head. He tuned his ears toward the high, melodic tin-kling and breathed out, his worry unraveling slightly under their influence, even though the harmonies were purely accidental.

Only three folk in Fahwyll could alter their spheres' pitch to tune them to a true harmony. Only three had enough mind-power to snag and hold more than a handful of heynim; to create measured harmonies and put them to use. One was Yornwey

4

the zjarn, who tuned her faleyn to heal a body's ill. The others were Throm and Bennoc, who tuned their faleyn in the fields at sowing and harvest: Throm, to the soil to encourage the crops; Bennoc, to the skies to bring fair weather. This trio held the biggest clusters in Fahwyll—almost two handfuls of heynim each. No others in the village could hold more than a half-dozen of the golden spheres, let alone control their chiming. Not even Tamborel's own mamma and pappa, as he found when he was old enough to ask.

"Sorry, but we're not able," Eleyna had answered, with a shake of her head that had set her little cluster a-bob and a-jingle.

"How can you be sure?"

"To tune a faleyn you need greater power than ours."

"Like the power Yornwey has, and Bennoc, and Throm? Is that why they're so important, Mamma?"

"Aye. We depend on faleyn for our lives—as you well know, Tam'shu."

He did indeed. Weren't the measured chimes such a vital part of life that the very world was named for them? *Alyafaleyn*, or Region of Harmonies. And weren't those who tuned them held in the highest esteem? Tamborel longed to be grown up and holding his own cluster, doing important work alongside Yornwey, and Bennoc, and Throm. "Are they the greatest folk in the world?"

Eleyna had found this amusing, though he'd been

quite serious. "In Fahwyll, at any rate. But they say that folk in Minavar trail swarms the length of our front path. Think how their faleyn would sound, Tam'shu. . . ."

Tamborel stole out from under the saba's shadow, scuffing his toe in the dusty garden path, drawn irresistibly toward the front gate by conflicting desires: to stay and learn what was going on and to slip off to the minnow brook. He pictured the older boys, their feet in the cool, swift currents, their stone crocks steely with minnows by now. He sidled on toward the gate, and had almost reached it when at last Eleyna noticed him. Frowning, she waved him back. "Inside, Tam'shu. I said you'll not go out today."

"But, Mamma, I want to be with Meynoc!" Meynoc, biggest of all the village boys. Good-natured Meynoc, who always suffered his company when the other boys ordered him away.

"Meynoc stays home, too, little one. Now go inside and be a good boy."

Tamborel retreated under the saba's shadow. Meynoc was indoors also? Hard to believe, but Eleyna always told the truth. During the last monsoons when he'd been taken with the moldy fever, she'd told him how truly bad it was, even after Hwyllum said that she should not. How Mistress Bider the herb wife had no remedy strong enough to break his fever. How they must call in Yornwey the zjarn. How Yornwey must tune her faleyn to his sickness, and how he must be a big boy, and bend his mind to help. Eleyna had frightened him, but, glad of the truth, he'd tried hard, fixing his ear on Yornwey's tinkling chimes. He'd slept, and awakened with the fever down, and his lungs clear.

A stray heyn floated past the saba, a tiny golden bubble almost within reach. A heyn still free, unsnagged, so long past the rains? In the days following the hard monsoons, the clear skies sparkled with them—fresh new ones, Eleyna said, although she couldn't say exactly where they came from, or why. Most were snagged over the city of Minavar. A few made it further east to Pridicum, the neighboring village. Of those, some very few, riding high, escaped to drift out Fahwyll-way. Had this one been tangled in a tree? Or caught in a rock cleft? Perhaps the wind had shaken it loose again, or a bird had dislodged it, maybe. Tamborel grabbed for it then hastily clasped his hands behind his back. What a baby, reaching for it physically! Embarrassed, he glanced to the women at the gate. To his relief, they had not noticed.

The heyn had floated on, its tantalizing notes receding on the breeze. Tamborel tried to fix his mind on it, to will it to him the way the big folk did, but without success. Wistfully, he watched it go, curving in a high arc, then dancing away over the low, flat rooftops on the gentle winds. He sighed, wishing he were old enough to snag a heyn and bind it to his mind with firm and steady purpose. But at five, he had a long wait. Even Meynoc, nearly thirteen years come harvest time had shown no signs of snagging yet.

As the dwindling sphere winked off into the blue, Tamborel's attention pricked. Over the women's mutter, and the tinkling of their heynim, he now heard new tones: stronger than Yornwey's, or Bennoc's, or Throm's, and deeper. In mounting excitement, he leaned out from under the saba's shadow, straining to hear. A stranger was approaching, bringing harmonies from outside!

As the chimes drew nearer, the watching women exclaimed, then fell quiet. Tamborel craned on tiptoe, striving vainly to peer over the garden wall. Oh, if only he were taller . . .

Tamborel ran to fetch a chair and climbed atop it. Now he could see all right, over the garden wall and along the street. Squeezing up his eyes against the noon glare, he made out two shapes stark against the Pridicum road. One was Meynoc's father, Bombrul, who should be in the grainfields at this hour. Beside him strode a stocky man of middle size and height: nothing remarkable about him—except that above his head swarmed the biggest golden cluster that Tamborel had ever seen. More: in among the tiny spheres swirled larger ones, sounding the deeper notes that he had heard. As the man strode past with Bombrul, Tamborel tried to count those bigger spheres, but there were too many, more than he had fingers, at any rate. Bending to the heynim's influence, he let go, remembering to breathe. Those larger spheres, Tamborel had never seen the like. No one in Fahwyll had such, not even Yornwey, or Bennoc, or Throm. Were the larger heynim more powerful than the little ones? he wondered. Did they do things the little ones could not? He longed to ask Eleyna these things, and also who the man was and why Meynoc's father had brought him to Fahwyll, but he dared not, for fear that Eleyna would banish him back inside.

The foreigner was past, and his golden heyn-cloud. The wondrous music faded in the distance. On a calculated risk, Tamborel scrambled down off the chair and ran to stand behind Eleyna, peering out.

"So that's Casinder," muttered Mistress Bider. "Bombrul must've run all the way to Pridicum to be fetching him so quick. Looks fair beat, poor man. And so he would, not being our best runner." The woman glanced to Eleyna. Everyone knew Hwyllum had the fastest legs and stoutest windpipe in the village.

"Serve him right," Mother Turner said. "He should've sent Hwyllum."

"The zjarn doesn't look the least bit winded," observed Mistress Bewly. "The way they boast about that man in Pridicum. No one can be that good. Though he does trail a bigger cluster than Yornwey's, I must admit."

Mother Turner nodded. "Let's hope it's more powerful, too. Rufina won't see the day out, else."

Tamborel's ears pricked. Rufina? Meynoc's mother, Bombrul's wife. She was ill? Is that why Bombrul had fetched Casinder? Why Meynoc had not come out to play? "Rufina must be *very* ill," he murmured anxiously.

Eleyna turned her head. "Just look at the bad boy!" she cried. "Go on in with you. There's no more here to see."

"But," wailed Tamborel, as his mother hustled him under the saba, pulling the lattice across, shutting them both inside. "Will Rufina die?"

Eleyna threw up her hands. "Hark at you!" she scolded. "What gives you such an idea! Did you not see Casinder just now? Did you not see his great cluster? He and Yornwey are going to tune their faleyn in augmentation so of course Rufina will be healed! Here, come away from that lattice and help me clean these bimbleberries. I've a pie to bake for tea!"

All afternoon, Tamborel longed to slip out to Meynoc's house, to hear the two zjarns tuning their faleyn together, in *augmentation* as his mother had called it. But Eleyna had not only closed the saba lattice. She had also latched all the saraba shutters, making the house dusky dark. Outside, the sun turned down, a dry breeze blew through the shutter slats. Men passed in the street, returning from the

10

fields. His father came in, subdued and disinclined to speak.

As Tamborel sat with his parents at supper, a neighbor called at their saba lattice. Tamborel jumped down to open it, but Eleyna barred his way. "Wait here, my lad," she said, and went out.

Presently she returned, looking grave.

"Who was it?" Tamborel burst out.

Eleyna only shook her head, exchanging looks with Hwyllum. After supper, the two of them went to stand under the saba, and closed the lattice behind them. Tamborel watched them speaking with their heads close, watched their heynim intermingling as was the way with family folk. Though they spoke low and kept their faces turned from him, Tamborel's keen ears caught enough. Rufina was no better. The two zjarns barely held her flame within its cup: if something were not done, and soon, Meynoc's mamma would die.

•2•

Eleyna shooed him into bed. "You've been a good boy, Tamborel. Now sleep, eh?" She picked up the lamp and went to his bedroom arch. As she made to slide his lattice closed, Tamborel struggled up from the covers. "Mamma!"

Eleyna paused, her hand on the lattice catch. "Yes, Tam'shu?"

"Will Rufina die?"

Eleyna came back, concerned. "My goodness, I hope not."

"Is it the moldy fever?" he asked, though he knew full well that it came only in the rainy season. His mother shook her head. "Then what?"

12

"She...has...poisons in her blood."

"Poisons!" Tamborel drew in his breath. "Did she eat something bad?"

Eleyna shook her head. "Don't worry, Tam'shu. She has two zjarns working for her now, and that must be powerful harmony."

Hwyllum came to the archway. "That young sprout's not bedded down yet?" He advanced into the room. "What is going on, Mamma?"

"Nothing, Hwyllum," Eleyna said.

"Oh? And what *nothing* is that, pray?"

Tamborel sank back onto his pillow. Trust Pappa to come in at this moment! He'd learn nothing further now.

"Tamborel was asking me about Rufina," Eleyna said.

"Indeed." Hwyllum folded his arms. "And so you fill a five-year-old with gory detail. Eleyna, he is much too young."

"Not too young to imagine the worst. He needs the truth—some of it, anyway."

Tamborel popped up again. "How could she get so sick so fast, Mamma?"

"She didn't, little one. It's been coming on for days. Mistress Bider gave her remedies, but she still got worse."

"But Meynoc never said. And he was fishing every day."

"Meynoc didn't know, Tam'shu." Eleyna stroked

back his hair. "Children don't know everything, not even big ones like Meynoc."

But now Rufina was so bad, they couldn't hide it any more, thought Tamborel. He eyed his parents suspiciously. "What if Rufina *does* die?"

Eleyna and Hwyllum exchanged glances. "She won't. She can't, Tam'shu. She's far too young and strong for death. Now down. We've told you all we know, just about."

Just about? Tamborel's fear spiked. "If she dies, what of Meynoc?"

"Tamborel, hush up." Eleyna thrust the lamp at Hwyllum and seized Tamborel in a fierce embrace, rocking him back and forth. Tamborel clung tightly in return. To lose one's mamma! What if *Eleyna* were to die?

At last, Eleyna released him and gently pushed him onto his pillow.

"You're a wonderful, caring boy, Tam'shu," she said, tucking him in again. "But you worry way beyond your years. Now: sleep. I have a vigil lamp to light." A votive lantern, like those already flickering under all the other sabas up and down the street, fervent wishes for Rufina's recovery.

Tamborel stared at the glow from his archway: lamplight reflecting down the passage from the middle room. His lattice cut dark bars across the light, making his room a cell. The corner shadows menaced now. If he closed his eyes and let himself go, might he die, too?

14

Clinging to wakefulness, Tamborel latched onto the comforting mix of noises from beyond his arch: the jingle of heynim, the quiet clatter of pots and dishes as his parents cleared up the kitchen, and the murmur of their voices. These formed his nightly lullaby. But this night he found no comfort in the talking. He tossed, and tossed again. Did Meynoc lie awake also? Oh, how he wished that he could help his friend's mamma!

A sudden rattle awoke him. Someone was at the saba lattice! What hour was it? How long had he been asleep? He reached his archway as his father opened the lattice, and saw that it was dark outside. Now came an urgent exchange of voices. Tamborel held still, straining his ears.

". . . if you leave now." That was Bombrul, breathless and a-roil. "Casinder says you might just catch it. It's our last hope, Hwyllum. Can you make it through the dark?"

Tamborel frowned. More talk, too low for him to hear. Hwyllum—leaving home and in the middle of the night? He snapped aside his lattice and ran out. The middle room was empty. Eleyna was with Bombrul in the kitchen, filling Hwyllum's water flask. "Tam'shu! What are you doing out of bed?"

At that moment, Hwyllum appeared, dressed for the fields. "Pappa!" Tamborel ran to him and seized his cape. "Don't go!"

15

"There now." Hwyllum struggled to disengage himself, setting his heynim a-swirl. "Eleyna! The boy is getting in a teasel!"

Eleyna bustled into the middle room, thrusting the flask and a food pack into Hwyllum's hand. "Young man, back to your room." She shooed Tamborel away and went with Hwyllum to the saba.

"No!" Tamborel ran after them. "Pappa, take me with you!" Tears came without warning, blurring his eyes.

Hwyllum paused by the saba lamp, looking stern. "Young man, even Bombrul cannot come. For I must run all night, and much of tomorrow. Your mamma will explain." Hwyllum patted his head, then strode to the gate with Bombrul. Tamborel watched the two men salute each other then take their leave, Bombrul turning toward his house, Hwyllum setting off into the dark at a trot, away from the village. Eleyna drew Tamborel back into the house. "You're trembling, Tam'shu. Come on, into bed with you, then I'll tell you where your pappa's gone, and why."

"No! No!" Tamborel broke away from Eleyna, raced off into his parents' room, and threw himself across the low, wide bed. "I stay with you tonight!"

"But Tam'shu," his mother protested. "You'll never sleep. Oh, well," she went on, as Tamborel clung to the covers. "Come on. But not too much talking, understand?" Tamborel climbed into his pappa's empty space and sat up, hugging his knees. "Pappa said you would explain," he insisted doggedly.

16

Eleyna was reaching to turn out the bedside lamp. With a sigh, she straightened up again. "Rufina is no better; neither Yornwey nor Casinder can heal her, not even with their faleyn tuned in augmentation."

"That's terrible!" Tamborel burst out. "But what is Pappa doing? Where's he gone?"

"The city road runs west of Pridicum. Casinder says a caravan is due to pass that way at dawn. Pappa is to meet it. There's someone in it who can fix Rufina."

"I know! I know who!" Tamborel waved his arms about. "Silwender—the High Zjarn of Minavar!" The greatest healer in the world who went out fixing everyone, except in the rains. Silwender lived in the *Hon'faleyn*, the Hall of Harmonies, where he taught the laws of harmony and the healing arts. Tamborel wished that he lived in the Hon'faleyn. Wished that he could watch Silwender every day tuning his faleyn. A *Grand Con-cat-en-ation*, Mamma had called it, a faleyn that size. He pictured Silwender a very giant, bigger than Filar the smith, striding by, trailing a swarm long as a comet's tail. Surely when the High Zjarn passed, everybody stopped and stared and listened, transfixed in his glistening web of chimes. Now Tamborel saw himself a zjarn with such a heynim cloud, saw the village people begging him to come and heal Rufina. He saw himself beside Rufina's bed, tuning a faleyn the like of which had never yet been heard: a Grand Con-cat-en-ation resounding clear to Pridicum!

"Did Yornwey study with Silwender, Mamma?"

"Oh, no, Tam'shu. Only the very gifted enter the Hon'faleyn."

"Poor Yornwey." Who could not help Rufina. Tamborel shuddered.

Eleyna reached for him and held him tight. "It's all right. Rufina will not die." Tamborel shrank into the shelter of his mother's arm. There was a place beyond the grainfields where the dead were buried. Most had died of old age, but there were some who had succumbed despite Mistress Bider's remedies and Yornwey's faleyn. The High Zjarn could have helped them, too. "What if Silwender doesn't come? He never has before."

"That's because we're too far off the beaten track, even farther out than Pridicum. Don't worry. Pappa will bring him, Tam'shu."

"Will I get to meet him?"

Eleyna sighed, reaching for the lamp. "I don't see how. But tell you what: tomorrow you may stand at the gate and watch him pass by."

18

·3·

After breakfast, as Tamborel went to run to the gate, Eleyna stopped him. "But you promised, Mamma!"

"It's too early, Tam'shu. Besides, I need your help right now."

Tamborel helped clear the table and wash the dishes, sighing loudly all the while. Not that he minded helping; he was just all of an itch to watch for his father—and for Silwender. When the dishes were put away and the house was swept and tidied, Eleyna set jars of aromatic oils to warm in the hearth. "Strong and fit as Pappa is, he's never run so far and fast. He'll be in sore need of rubbing down, Tam'shu." Pungent odors filled the house, making his eyes water. Around noon, Eleyna filled the laundry copper, and lit a fire beneath it to heat water for Hwyllum's bath. Tamborel stared. Two fires burning now—at the summer's height! The copper boiled and steam ran down the walls. He fled to the saba, pressing his face to the stones, seeking the slightest breeze, while his mother, strands of hair plastered to her crimson cheeks, labored on. At last she called:

"Go to the gate now, Tam'shu. Pappa should be coming soon!"

Freed at last, Tamborel raced to the gate and looked down the street toward the Pridicum road. He stood there for an age, but Hwyllum did not appear. Tamborel grew anxious. Could Pappa have come to harm? The shadows lengthened. Then, toward dusk, Tamborel became aware of the strangest feeling. His skin prickled, the hairs stood out on his arms, and he felt a flash of energy, the sort he sometimes experienced after a rich, sugary pudding. Tamborel rubbed his arms expectantly. Something was in the air.

But what?

Up the road, about a mile away: a tiny puff of dust.

"Mamma!" he shouted, and ran. His body felt so light he scarcely could feel the ground. Behind him, folk streamed out, shading their eyes against the falling sun. Reaching the village boundary, Tamborel pulled up. And then he heard it: a wash of distant chimes. So that was it! He had felt their vibrations even before his ears could pick them up!

Tamborel strove to see through the growing dust cloud. Nearer it swirled, nearer, nearer. . . . The chimes grew louder: such a full, rich sound, even at this distance. Folk pushed in front of him, edging him aside so that he had to fight to keep his place.

Everyone went still.

Two shapes emerged from the dust cloud: Hwyllum, staggering along beside a beast with serpent neck and bulging belly atop four high, spindly legs: a qarl, that the Minavar merchants rode when they came to bid for grain at harvest. Perched cross-legged upon the qarl's box saddle was a man. He was very small, and old, with straggly silver hair and beard. But in spite of his frail appearance, he rode easy with the beast's bumpy gait, his right hand loose on the reins. His pale blue robe hung on him in folds; in his left hand he held a small blue parasol, gold-fringed, although the sun's rays were almost horizontal now, and slicing underneath it.

Above the dust cloud swirled the old man's heynim like a golden halo circling the sun. Tamborel stood spellbound—until Hwyllum, drawing level with him, staggered, and almost fell.

"Pappa'shu!"

Tamborel dashed forward, but stronger hands reached out, bearing Hwyllum up. Silwender leaned out from his lofty perch and Tamborel met the old man's eye. He stared, caught in the High Zjarn's watery appraisal. Then the qarl was lurching onward

21

down the street, and the man was past, his vast swarm churning high above the people's heads.

Tamborel watched the procession dwindle up the street, feeling the pull of those chimes. Even in their idle state, circling untuned, he felt their latent power. Before he knew it, he was trotting after, his father forgotten.

"Tam'shu!" Eleyna's voice brought him up short. "Where do you think you're going?" Men were carrying Hwyllum through their garden gate. What could Tamborel do but accompany his mother into the house?

Those heynim! Those wondrous harmonies! Tamborel's whole body was tight with desire. At that very moment Silwender was tuning up a Grand Concatenation and here he was, stuck inside stone walls, no hope that the sound would carry this far. His only chance *ever* to hear such chiming!

Tamborel helped Eleyna fill a bowl with warm water and wet a pile of cloths, picturing Silwender in Rufina's chamber all the while. How would that wondrous swarm fit into one small space? he wondered, as Eleyna knelt to tend his father's feet.

They were so swollen that Eleyna had to cut away his shoes. Slowly, tenderly, she peeled off the leg bindings. They came off caked in blood and grit and sticking to the flesh. Surely it must hurt, thought Tamborel, as his mother eased them off. But his father never once complained or even flinched: it was not his way. At last, Eleyna handed Hwyllum a herbal cup to sip, and slid his bloody feet into a bowl of Mistress Bider's cleansing balm.

Tamborel watched guiltily. Bad boy, wanting to slip away to hear the High Zjarn's music with his father in this state. He followed Eleyna into the kitchen. "Pappa looks very bad."

"Well, he's lost so much fluid, you see, Tam'shu," Eleyna said. "And his muscles are wasted. But with a hot soak, a herbal rub, and a good night's sleep he'll be fine again come morning." Eleyna hugged Tamborel, stroking his hair. "You're a dear, good boy. You worked so hard for me today. I couldn't have managed without you. Now come, help me fill your pappa's bath. Then it's time for bed."

The moment Eleyna slid his lattice closed, Tamborel slid out of bed and ran to his saraba. The window hole was small, and round, and needed but one shutter. Set into the side of the house, it faced the narrow space between dwellings. Outside noises did not carry well into this sleeping chamber: an asset—until now.

Tamborel pressed his ear to the shutter slats, straining for the slightest sound of chiming. Nothing, as he had expected. Oh, to think of all that he was missing! He pictured Rufina lying on her bed, her skin clammy and cold, her brow beaded with sweat, the way his had been with the moldy fever. Yornwey's faleyn had flowed through him like cool spring water, washing the fever from his body. Lucky Rufina, to feel the flood of great Silwender's harmonies! Well, he thought, trying to make the best of it, even if he couldn't *hear* the chimes, could he perhaps *feel* them as he had before?

Tamborel went still, holding his breath, setting his mind on that shining, gold cloud. All at once, he felt the air quiver. His skin goosed up as though from a sudden draft. Then his whole body went light and trembly, as it had before. Elated, Tamborel wanted to jump up and down but knew that he must stay quiet still or lose everything. He let his breath out cautiously—then lost focus anyhow at a quick new thought:

What if he unlatched his shutter, climbed out the saraba—and ran to Rufina's house? Mamma and Pappa need never know, not if he waited until after they had gone to sleep. And no one would see him in the dark. Tamborel shivered with excitement. Oh, the danger of it! He'd never dare—would he?

Footsteps sounded in the passage outside. Mamma, coming to see if he was asleep. Tamborel ran, dove under the covers just as she reached his archway lattice. He listened to her steps recede, heard his parents in the bedchamber next door. He sat up straight now, watching the glow on the wall outside. It faded. Mamma had turned out her lamp.

Tamborel waited, his heart racing. He must decide, now.

There came a rustle as his parents settled down.

Then silence. Slowly, Tamborel set his feet to the floor. Then he tiptoed to the saraba and inched up the shutter latch. Gingerly, he let it down and swung the slatted frame open. The neighbor's house was dark, a low, squat bulk against the deep night sky. Tamborel pulled himself up onto the curving sill and peered down. It wasn't too far to the ground, an easy climb to get back in. Gingerly, he swung his legs over. Then, bracing himself, he tumbled out onto the turf below.

·4·

Tamborel crouched, tense, then, when nothing happened, he picked himself up and stole around to the front of the house and out through the gate. There, he paused again, wavering. He hadn't dreamed it would be so dark. And Rufina's house was way down the far end of the street, past the well at the Y-fork, and as far again, almost to where the cobbles gave way to stony track at the grainfields' edge. That was the way men trod to and from work each day, and where he took the path to the brook.

He looked into the darkness fearfully. The street seemed so different now. And what if Mamma woke up and found him gone! Bad boy, to run out like this, knowing it was wrong. But he *had* to hear Silwender's chimes!

Tamborel pattered off down the street, his night-shirt catching at his legs. The deep, round cobble-stones hurt the soles of his feet, making him wish that he'd put on his shoes. He glanced fearfully to either side. The tiny flames under each house saba burned like eyes, watching him.

At the Y-fork, a bullfrog croaked from the bottom of the well and Tamborel cried aloud. A nearby gate creaked on its hinges and he almost turned and ran but just then the tingling began again, tugging him on.

He was almost there when he heard voices. People stood by Rufina's gate, watching the house. Mistress Bider, for one; Mother Turner, for another. Oh, oh, they'd find him out for sure, he told himself, but he couldn't back down now. He ducked sideways through the nearest gateway and ran to the rear of the house. From there, he made his way through the remaining backyards to Rufina's, under the pull of the chimes.

Light blazed through every saraba, cutting between the shutter slats. Loud chimes beat the night air, while single notes tumbled in and out, a snatch of melody repeated over and over. Tamborel listened until he found himself humming along. The notes climbed. Now each tone took on a sort of echo way up high that set Tamborel's ears a-whirr.

He moved forward, drawn by those weird over-tones, around the side of the house, coming at last to Rufina's chamber.

Grasping the saraba sill, he pulled himself up and peered inside.

Spheres swarmed, so thick that Tamborel could scarcely make out Rufina in bed and Silwender standing beside her. And the sound! *Too much*! Letting go, Tamborel fell into a heap under the saraba sill. And there he lay, his hands clapped to his ears. The chiming swelled until it hurt. Surely his head would burst! He curled up, terrified. He couldn't move. He couldn't even call out—and if he did, who would hear him over all that sound?

All at once, somewhere deep within him, some-thing unraveled, and slowly, Tamborel took his hands away and let the sounds engulf him. There came a clap of thunder, then a rushing of wind—or was it the gush of floodwater? Colors swirled, music rolled. Then all was dark again. Perhaps he slept awhile. Next he knew, the chimes were slow and quiet, like a low, slow pulse. Tamborel cracked an almighty yawn, then stretched. He could stand up now, he found. Reaching shakily on tiptoe, he peeped through Rufina's shutter slats.

The swarm was slowly circling around the cham-ber, the old man in the middle. And Bombrul was pulling the archway lattice aside.

Tamborel turned away and made for home. The

28

watchers by the gate had gone. The streets were utterly deserted. It seemed that the village, the whole world had slowed, and gone into a deep slumber.

He reached his front gate in a daze, climbed back through his saraba and closed the shutter. Then, falling into bed, Tamborel went to sleep at once.

When he awoke, it was light. He came up slowly into wakefulness, remembering. He thought of the wondrous sounds rolling over him, swamping his senses, and the marvelous play of colors swirling around him in the dark. He remembered how at first he had been frightened. "Right after those funny echoes," he told himself, pulling on his clothes. "Those really high notes that hurt my ears." Tamborel had never heard their like. Eleyna might know what they were—but it would not be wise to ask her, he decided, as he went in to breakfast.

His mamma kissed him, set out his bowl, seemingly in great spirits. "You're late, Tam'shu. Never mind, everyone in this village is up late today. Your pappa's not yet even awake. What is that you're humming?"

He was humming? Indeed he was: a catch from the High Zjarn's Grand Concatenation—but he could hardly tell Eleyna. "How is Rufina, Mamma?"

"Much better, Mistress Bider says. She's in a deep and healing sleep. You remember how that was, Tam'shu?"

"Oh, yes," Tamborel said, but he wasn't thinking of Yornwey and the moldy fever. He sighed, recalling the sudden release at the height of the chiming. It occurred to him then that Silwender would soon be leaving. "Can I watch the High Zjarn ride out, Mamma?"

"Sorry, Tam'shu. He's already gone."

"No!" Tamborel eyed Eleyna in dismay. "How could he in the dark?"

"Hush." Eleyna gestured toward her bedchamber. "Guides came for him, they say. Pity you missed him, but he has a way to go. It was a big favor to break his journey and come so far off his regular route. Maybe when she's well enough, Rufina can tell us how it was to feel such power, eh, Tam'shu? Would you like that?"

Tamborel looked away. Those chimes, he had felt them also. Felt their influence still. He should be out of sorts to find Silwender gone. But he was too... peaceful, somehow. He wondered how Meynoc had felt so close to the wondrous chiming. Now Tamborel had an urge to seek him out. "Is Pappa better today?" He glanced sideways to Eleyna. "Will you be needing me?"

Eleyna laughed aloud. "Eat your breakfast and wash your face," she said. "Your fishing crock is waiting by the saba."

When Tamborel got to the brook, Meynoc was not there. He stood, uncertain as to what to do. Maybe if he hung around, Meynoc would come. The other big boys eyed him sourly, but suffered him to stay—at a distance. Tamborel dipped his net into the stream, watching the others sideways. They looked subdued, even furtive, and they kept their voices unusually low.

". . . she'll stay abed the full two months more, my mamma says. She'll lose it, else," said one, a boy named Rafil.

"Better she did, my mamma says. She wouldn't want to keep a thing that almost killed her," said another, Fodir.

"Hush." A third looked Tamborel's way. "Little crocks have large ears. He'll tell, and we'll be whipped."

Tamborel turned from them, his ears burning. The boys talked on, their voices rising and falling in waves. ". . . Meynoc said his mamma wants it bad. He said it's not the baby's fault his mamma got blood poison," Rafil remarked, his voice coming back up to its normal shout.

"I said hush!" Fodir warned. "We're not supposed to know yet that babies grow inside their mother. . . ."

Tamborel's hands tightened on the handle of his fishing net. They were talking about Rufina. And a baby. He stared fixedly at the bright, swirling water, his cheeks aflame. He knew that babies grew inside their mother, hadn't Eleyna explained last year when he couldn't help but see how Mistress Bider had grown so fat? Although, now her baby was born,

Mistress Bider was not a whit smaller. In fact, she was larger, now, if anything. . . .

A baby—growing inside Rufina! A baby, poisoning its mother's blood? Tamborel frowned. How, when it was not yet born? Tamborel sat, his net forgotten. Along the bank, the boys scrambled up, gathered their gear, and trooped away. Sighing, Tamborel withdrew his net, picked up his empty crock and trudged home after them, thinking of the child as yet unborn. "Poor baby," he murmured to himself. It had suffered just as much as Rufina, had almost died along with her. And here it was, taking all the blame.

Tamborel halted in his tracks.

Poor baby?

The unborn child had suffered, yes. Had almost died. *But it had also felt the full force of the High Zjarn's healing chimes!*

Part Two

·5·

Tamborel scuffed his toes impatiently by the gate, watching the saba. He looked along the street toward Rufina's, where they were supposed to be going. "If ever they're ready." He glanced in the other direction, westward to the Pridicum road. One year to the very day since Silwender came in a cloud of dust to heal Rufina. Now they were to mark it in a very special way.

"Tam'shu!" Eleyna called out behind him. "Do you want your good clothes dirty before we're out the gate? Come inside!"

Sighing, Tamborel obeyed. Eleyna had been fussing with her dress and hair for an hour now. "The

35

Gathering's started. What if they're naming the baby already?"

"And Pappa the Grand Mareschal in charge of Ceremony? Not to mention that he's also to be her father-mentor. They'll wait for us, don't worry. You want to share a big secret, Tam'shu? Come." Eleyna beckoned him inside.

Secret? Tamborel hurried into his parents' bed-chamber. Eleyna went to the glass and began pinning up her tawny curls. She looked so very beautiful today, Tamborel observed proudly. In her long yellow gown that she kept for high holidays and with her hair piled high, she stood almost as tall as Hwyllum. "What secret?"

Tamborel's father was over by the linen chest.

"Show him, Pappa," Eleyna said.

"See." Hwyllum took something up off the chest top: a carved wooden box, inlaid with bits of brown shell. He put the box to Tamborel's ear and shook it. From within came a high, thin tinkling. Tamborel looked up. "A *heyn*?" Hwyllum raised the box lid for Tamborel to peep inside. Yes, a heyn, lying like a tiny golden egg in a blue velvet nest.

"Where's it from, Pappa? What's it doing in the box?"

"Silwender sent it. It's for Rufina's baby, to mark her naming day."

"The High Zjarn asked Pappa to present it, isn't that grand?" Eleyna stuck a flower pin through her top-knot, eyeing its angle critically. "Because he saved Rufina's life, I'm sure."

"And the baby's," Tamborel added. He eyed his father proudly now. Hwyllum was the hero of the hour. As a consequence, they'd made him Grand Mareschal of this Gathering, although he was not a man for public speaking. In addition, Rufina and Bombrul had asked him to be the baby's father-mentor. Now this great honor bestowed on him by the High Zjarn himself. The day was getting better by the minute!

Hwyllum wrapped the box in a napkin and tucked it into Eleyna's flower-filled basket. Eleyna set down her hairbrush and gave her skirts a final twirl. "Ready." She picked up the basket and at long last they set off down the street. Tamborel kept looking at the basket, thinking of the shining, golden secret inside. That baby—just ten months born and owning a heyn already, without ever having done a thing!

The yard was crowded. Rufina sat in the matron's bower, receiving guests and gifts. A yard or so away, the baby lay sleeping in a child-pen, shaded by her own small canopy decked with streamers.

Tamborel gazed around at everything—especially the clusters of heynim dancing over the assembly. He loved Gatherings, when all the spheres in the village were brought into one place. He closed his eyes, savoring the chimes: bubbling, bouncing, golden rivulets, swirling like the currents in the minnow brook with the movements of their owners' heads. He heard someone laugh, a quick burst of notes. To his left, Yornwey walked by: he'd know her soothing harmonies anywhere.

"Here, Tam'shu." Tamborel opened his eyes. Eleyna stood before him, her flower basket on her arm. She slipped the heyn box from the basket and into his hand. "Hold it—careful now. Don't let anyone see it until we say."

Tamborel watched her walk away. He, entrusted with the shining, golden secret! He slid the box inside his jacket and crossed his arms protectively. Lucky baby, to get such a gift. Tamborel made for the baby's pen.

Awake now, the child was sitting up, surrounded by Mother Turner and a bunch of other wives. "Kutchy-coo." Mother Turner leaned down. "Pretty one, your mamma should be proud."

"Grateful, more like," Mistress Bider muttered, glancing fondly to her own child hugging her skirts: Tancey, who was two years old now. "Poisoning poor Rufina like that! Lucky she didn't die."

Mother Turner frowned. " 'Tweren't the new baby's fault Rufina took sick like that. Besides, she nearly died, too."

"They say Yornwey told Rufina not to have another child after Meynoc."

"There! You see?" a third wife hissed. "That's what comes of ignoring our healer's advice: a little monster!"

38

"Gah," the little monster said, screwing up her face and reaching out toward them.

"Look! You see that scowl? She knows what you're saying. I'd watch my tongue if I were you or she'll give you the evil eye." Mistress Bider scooped up Tancey and the women moved away.

Monster? Evil eye? Tamborel went sore inside, as though he'd been physically hurt. The meanness! He wondered why they came to the Gathering at all! Tamborel edged forward, peering into the pen, seizing a rare chance to study the child alone and at such close quarters. Her eyes were large, and round, and a deep, clear blue. Her hair was wiry as a frytt-burr, and dark, like Bombrul's. As he stood there, sizing her up, she upped onto her hands and knees and scrambled nimbly toward him. "Gah," she said. Reaching the place where he stood, she grasped the side of the pen, pulled herself up and clung unsteadily. "Gah. Uh-gah."

Tamborel leaned down and looked into her eyes.

Their gaze held, and in that moment, Tamborel thought of the night, one whole year before, when he'd lain beneath Rufina's sill, overwhelmed by Silwender's chimes. You, you, he told her silently, you heard them, too. *Felt* them! And as he thought it, he knew then that she was going to be special— though not any *monster*!

Tamborel glanced around to see that no one observed, then to the treasure inside his jacket. "Don't let anyone see it," Eleyna had told him, expressly. But surely that didn't mean the baby. After all, it was going to be hers any minute now. He slipped the napkin-covered box from under his coat and held it out. "Here: you've a gift from Silwender, High Zjarn of Minavar! Listen." He shook the box by her ear, starting soft chimes within. Letting go the side of the pen, the baby grabbed for the box with such force that she toppled over backward, her feet in the air. "Gah! Uh-*gah*!" She rolled, was pulling herself back on her feet in an instant, her eyes fixed on the box.

Tamborel slipped the box quickly behind his back. "In a bit, you'll get it in a bit," he said. The baby sat down with a bump and began to bawl.

Hwyllum came up, looking flustered. "It's naming time. I must call the Gathering to order. You have the box?"

"Yes, Pappa!" Tamborel held it out. "Pappa, the baby knows—"

"Later." Hwyllum pushed the box away. "Keep it till I say. Come on."

At Hwyllum's signal, a bell sounded, and everyone gathered around Rufina's bower. Tamborel went to stand by Hwyllum, the box behind his back. Through the sudden stillness, the baby's cries rang out, strident, demanding.

"Good gracious," Rufina murmured anxiously. "Whatever can be wrong?"

40

"Not to worry," Mother Turner reassured her. "Children surely do pick their times."

Cerie, Rufina's sister, who was to be the mother-mentor, lifted the baby from the pen, patting her back, trying to hush her squalling.

Tamborel watched, brimming with guilt. His fault, *his*, for showing her Silwender's heyn. But how was he to know that it would set her off like that? There were heynim all around her and she'd not gone after them in this way.

Hwyllum cleared his throat. "We are gathered here," he began, then started over, vying with the baby's wails. "We are gathered here on this joyous occasion to name this child. As you all know, this is past the proper time for naming. But in view of the remarkable event that preceded her birth, namely, the coming of the great High Zjarn of Minavar, it was decided to hold the Gathering on this, the anniversary of Silwender's visit. Now let us begin." Hwyllum turned to Bombrul. "Who is father to this child?" he called loudly. As if everyone didn't know that perfectly well, thought Tamborel.

Bombrul moved to stand beside Hwyllum. "I am."

"And who, the mother?"

"I am." Rufina spoke up shyly. Then she went on, speaking the mother's part. "Who will be mother-mentor to our child?"

"I, Cerie of Fahwyll," Cerie said, jiggling the baby,

who, mercifully, was falling quiet. "My hearth and heart shall evermore be open to her need."

Now Bombrul spoke the father's part. "Who'll be father-mentor to our child?" Everyone turned to Hwyllum expectantly.

"I, Hwyllum of Fahwyll." He took the baby gingerly from Cerie's arms. "My hearth and heart shall evermore be open to her need."

Tamborel let out a deep sigh of satisfaction. The grandness of it all!

Bombrul spoke again. "Now who will say our new child's chosen name?"

"I will," Hwyllum answered. "As Grand Mareschal of this Gathering, I do proclaim that from henceforth this child shall be called Caidrun."

Caidrun: gift of healing! Tamborel gazed triumphantly around. There! That should fix them. Rufina took back her child, smiling at the guests. Now Hwyllum took the heyn box from Tamborel, unwrapped it, and held it up. "From Silwender, High Zjarn: a naming gift for Caidrun." He raised the lid a slit and carefully withdrew the heyn between thumb and forefinger. The tiny golden globe sparkled in the sunlight, and its high, tinkling music danced.

"Oh!" Rufina cried amid the general exclamations. "Why would he send our Caidrun such a precious thing?"

Bombrul took it carefully from Hwyllum's hand. "Precious thing for precious child. Let no one doubt it, see!" He held it high for everyone to admire. The sun caught it, making it flash. At that, Caidrun exclaimed and reached toward it. "Look!" Rufina cried. "She seeks to snag it already!"

The people laughed indulgently. "Indeed, she is a genius born."

Behind Tamborel, Mistress Bider murmured. "Such nonsense. We all have had to keep our heynim out of our children's reach. All babies of that age grab for everything that moves."

"And everything that shines," Mistress Bewly agreed. "How many bead necklaces did I lose to my Tolas's clutching fingers!"

Tamborel jumped up and down, scarce able to contain himself. Were they blind? Rufina was right. The heyn was not just any old bright thing to catch her attention. "Caidrun *knows* that heyn!" he muttered fiercely.

Cups were filled and passed around. Even Tamborel got a thimbleful.

Hwyllum raised his cup. "To Caidrun!"

"To Caidrun!" everyone shouted, and drank. Tamborel wiped his mouth with the back of his hand. Now Hwyllum called for musicians and the folk to begin a slow chain dance, hopping and shuffling through the house and around the outside walls, to weave the baby's new name into her small world, and with it great good fortune. They set Caidrun down inside her pen, and, stowing the heyn box in

Rufina's bower, Rufina and Bombrul took hands. Guests lined up behind them, men behind Bombrul, women behind Rufina, hand to shoulder, stretching back, then the columns moved away to stately pipe and tambour, around the house and out of sight. Those not so limber stayed behind, fanning themselves against the heat. "Such a waste," complained Mistress Bewly. "That so fine and precious a thing will lie shut away for so long—ten more years, at least!"

"Lucky little mite," another woman sniffed. "To own a heyn from birth."

"*Lucky?*" Mother Turner shook her head. "To miss snagging her first heyn? I well remember mine. Just thirteen, I was. I were that excited I let it go." Now they were off, all talking at once.

". . . my boy Rafil's almost old enough to snag his first. . . ."

". . . fifteen years old before I held on to one, and then it . . ."

". . . sister only twelve, and snagging three. But could I catch a one?"

Tamborel could keep quiet no longer. "Caidrun will snag hers quite soon, you'll see. She's reaching out already."

The women laughed merrily. "Get away with you, young Tamborel," Mother Turner said. "No mere child can snag a heyn."

"Caidrun will. She's special."

"Special?" Mother Turner looked quizzical. "How so, young man?"

"She felt the High Zjarn's power before she was even born."

"Well!" Mistress Bider cried. "Hark at him! What does he know about such things?"

Mother Turner laughed good-naturedly. "You must admit he's quite the hero, standing up for little Missy there."

"By the skies, what are you doing, boy? Hanging around, listening to wives gossip!" Hwyllum strode up, looking severe. "Get away with you, go find Meynoc."

"But Pappa—"

Hwyllum shooed him away.

At the corner of the house, Tamborel paused and glanced back to where the baby sat underneath her canopy. "Caidrun." He tested it out aloud.

If Pappa was her father-mentor, was not he, Tamborel, now her brother, in a way? That thought pleased him greatly, having no blood sibling at home. "I know you're special, Caidrun. I'll look after you, I promise," he said, then ran to find the older boys.

·6·

The next day, Tamborel tried to make his parents understand what had really happened. "I shook the box at Caidrun and she grabbed at it. She knew that it was hers—that was why she made so much fuss."

"You had no business showing it to her, after your mamma told you to keep it hid," Hwyllum said, frowning. "You were a disobedient boy."

"That was some tantrum, though," Eleyna said. "She looks set to be quite a mettlesome miss. I'd say Rufina's going to have her hands full."

Tamborel saw his chance. "I can help. I'll play with Caidrun while Rufina gets her work done."

Eleyna shot him a look. "What? You—serve as

46

Caidrun's nursemaid? Why, you don't know the child. You've hardly ever seen her."

But I do know her, thought Tamborel. Caidrun's special, even if you cannot see it. "I want to mind her."

Hwyllum snorted. "What—going on seven and asking to play with a baby only ten months old? I never heard such nonsense. What's gotten into you?"

Tamborel looked down. All he knew was, now he'd seen Caidrun close up, he wanted to be with her, to look after her. That, having shared a singular experience with her, even before she was born, he felt connected to her, somehow. He saw again those wide blue eyes on him. She'd taken to him, and meaning well, he'd shown her the heyn box, only to snatch it away. His fault that she'd cried and spoiled her naming ceremony. "I want to help."

"Then help your mamma," Hwyllum said. "Or lend me a hand in the field."

"He's lonely, Pappa." Eleyna went to give Tamborel a hug. "He has no one of his own age to play with; no brother or sister of his own."

Tamborel seized his chance. "Now, I have. If Pappa is Caidrun's father-mentor, that makes me a sort of brother, doesn't it?"

Eleyna laughed. "You must admit he makes a point." She released Tamborel, stroked his hair. "You're a very counselor, Tam'shu. I'll speak to Rufina and maybe she'll let you visit and see how it works out."

For the rest of the summer, Tamborel dropped by Rufina's yard each day to mind Caidrun in her pen. He took along a rag doll that Eleyna had made, and a set of small, smooth building stones that he'd culled from the shallows of the brook. He danced the doll, showed her how to build with the stones, even though Caidrun's chief amusement was to knock them down and scatter them again. When she tired of playing, he sang songs to her, little game chants like the one the older boys used in a ring game to pick the middle one. "One ear of grain, two ears of grain, three and another make four. . . ." He made up tales about the creatures of the grainfields. He also told stories that the grain merchants brought from outside, scary tales about the Jagged Mountains west of Minavar; a desolate, forbidden range where mist wraiths danced at the edge of the world. He told his own favorites, scary tales of the man who was swallowed up by the peaks. Of the girl who danced with the mist wraiths and fell under their spell. And of the foolish boy who went to the mountains in the monsoons and was washed into the earth like salt. Caidrun listened, rapt, curled in the crook of his arm.

"Away with you, Tamborel," Rufina said, pretending to scold. "It's a good job she's too young to understand, or she'd be keeping us up of nights with nightmares. But I declare, she seems quite taken with your stories and your singing. Meynoc, her own brother, can't occupy her so well as that."

48

After harvesting, as the days drew in, Rufina moved the pen inside. And Tamborel continued to visit, no more pining after Meynoc and the rest. Here, at Rufina's, he was welcome. No "Go be a good boy." Or "Run off, you're too small to go with us." The moment Tamborel stepped through the saba, Caidrun shrieked with delight, and her joy at seeing him was nectar to his spirit.

Now Rufina let Caidy out of the pen, under Tamborel's watchful care. Holding both her hands firmly, he walked her patiently around the room until one day she let go and took her first steps unaided. "Rufina! Quick! Caidrun's walking!"

"Uh-gah!" cried Caidrun, and raised a fist in glee.

"Well, look at that!" cried Rufina, and Caidrun promptly sat down.

From then on, there was no stopping her. Every day there was something new to marvel at. Then she began to speak single words: *Pappa, Mamma. Ay-nock.* And, to Tamborel's delight, *Brel*—her name for him.

Tamborel did note one strange thing: while other babies grew used to heynim, coming finally to ignore them, Caidrun seemed to find them ever more attractive. At times, when in a cranky mood, she would just sit and yell for Rufina to come so that she could listen to her mother's cluster. On those occasions, only those high, thin notes would restore Caidrun's good humor.

The first rains set in, heralding the monsoons. Now

when Tamborel visited Rufina's house, Caidrun latched onto him, trotted after him from room to room—except when Rufina was by. Then Caidrun clamored to be lifted up, so that she could grab for her mother's heynim.

"Look at that," Meynoc said, laughing with brotherly pride. "When there's a heyn in the offing, she has no time for us, Tamborel."

One afternoon, as Tamborel arrived at Meynoc's house, Rufina burst from the kitchen, Caidrun in her arms. "Here," Rufina said, setting Caidrun down in the middle of the floor. "She's after my chimes again. I'll never get the supper made at this rate. Mind her, you boys. Keep her occupied."

Meynoc shrugged. "How, Mamma?"

Caidrun clung to Rufina's skirts, wailing loudly. "Oosiks, *oosiks*!"

"Music?" Rufina turned to Tamborel. "Will you sing to her?"

In front of Meynoc? Tamborel looked down. "I can't, just now."

Caidrun began to struggle and kick, threatening a full tantrum. "Oh, dear." Rufina grew desperate. "I know." She dashed into her bedchamber, came back brandishing Silwender's gift. "Here, Meynoc, jiggle this at her. Make sure the catch stays closed—and don't let her have hold of it." As she hurried back to the kitchen, Caidrun opened her mouth to bawl, but before she could utter a sound, Meynoc shook the

50

box, starting the chimes within. Caidrun stopped absolutely still. Then she turned on Meynoc, her face radiant. "Oosiks, Ay-nock."

Meynoc shoved the box at Tamborel. "Here. You take charge." He threw himself back into his seat and put his feet up.

Tamborel could scarce believe his luck. He hadn't seen the heyn box since Caidrun's naming party. It was smaller than he remembered, and it had gotten dull. He buffed it on his sleeve, shining up the brown shell inlay, then he shook it, listening to the tiny chimes.

"Brel!" Caidrun teetered toward him, smiling, arms outstretched.

"Go on," Meynoc urged. "Shake it again. Let her hear."

"But—" Too late, Tamborel realized that this was the naming day all over again. He couldn't let Caidrun have the box, and this was going to make her cry—or worse, start a full-blown tantrum.

As Caidrun squeezed up her face to yell, Tamborel held out the box and shook it lightly. "Listen, Caidy."

Caidrun canceled the yell, grabbed for the box and missed.

Meynoc clapped his hands, delighted. "That's it! Go for it, Caidy!"

What could Tamborel do but hold out the box again, then snatch it away, only just in time. To his relief, Caidrun found this amusing. Now they were off, playing tag with the heyn box; Caidrun trying to seize it, Tamborel keeping it just out of reach. At last, she got it, catching Tamborel off guard. He tugged, she held on, and they toppled sideways, shrieking with laughter, the box clutched between them.

"Hey!" Rufina hustled from the kitchen and took the box away. "You go too far! I meant for the box to be shaken, Tamborel, not used as a toy! And you, Meynoc: lazy boy, just sitting there. Why did you not stop them?"

Meynoc only grinned. "You should see Caidrun, Mamma. She's so quick and strong. And determined, too."

"Enough! You'll turn your sister's head," she said, looking pleased even so. "You, Tamborel, run off home now. It's almost suppertime: your mamma will be wondering where you are."

The monsoons passed, the skies lightened, and Hwyllum went out to the muddy grainfields, cutting drainage lines and preparing the soil for spring tillage. Now folk started looking upward, watching for heynim. One week into the tilling, the first stragglers were sighted: a modest cluster, barely more than the fingers of one hand. Now began the yearly scramble when villagers made good their losses—for the heynim did not last forever. After a number of seasons, they fell prey to wet and wind. Their luster faded, the chimes fell silent; they lost their buoyancy

and tumbled to the ground. Then they were respect-
fully buried, and replaced.

The snagging over, folk went back to work, for
there was always much to do after the monsoons, in
both house and field.

Hwyllum took Tamborel to help him hoe along the
irrigation channels and pile uprooted weeds for com-
post. The work was tiring, but Tamborel did not
mind, for bigger boys were working, too. It was good
to toil in full view of his elders. And it marked his
age: seven now, going on eight. Now on days off,
they did not object so much to his tagging along.

The summer days whisked by, and suddenly, there
was Rufina, calling with an invitation to the first anniversary of Caidrun's naming.

It should have been a small affair: handful of children, simple gifts, modest feast. But somehow, it
turned into another full Gathering. Hwyllum did not
approve. "It sets Caidrun apart," he said. "And I will
say as much."

"Now, Hwyllum," Eleyna said. "The child was set
apart even before she was born. Besides, you're not
her father, so hold your peace."

"That I shan't. Am I not her mentor? I have some
say in her rearing. If Bombrul and Rufina aren't careful, the child will grow up spoiled."

Whether Hwyllum spoke or no, the Gathering was
held. The day dawned hot and dry and sunny, just as

on the naming day one year before. Folk went to Rufina's house, with gifts and dishes for the feast. In the center of the gift table, amid the toys and pretty clothes, was the heyn box. "To remind us all of the honor that Silwender did our girl," Rufina explained proudly.

Tamborel was drawn toward the small brown box. As though, having had charge of it twice now, it partly belonged to him. The grownups made speeches, Rufina showed Caidrun her gifts: straw dolls, woven throwing balls, a wooden cup and dish, smocks, petticoats, and pinafores, as became a child almost two years old. But when Caidrun caught sight of the heyn box, she wanted nothing else. She grasped the edge of the table, pulled herself on tiptoe, demanding for her mamma to hand it over. "No, little one." Rufina moved it out of range. "You must wait until you're older."

Caidrun puckered up her face to cry.

Oh, thought Tamborel. She remembered the game they'd played way back before the monsoons, when Tamborel had shaken the box and teased her. She had also held that box, for a moment, and likely remembered that, too.

Caidrun began to yell. "Oosiks, *oosiks!*"

"You want music, Caidy? Come, hear mamma's chimes." Rufina tried to draw Caidrun away, but she clung to the table, in full-throttled squall.

"I'll put it inside," Bombrul said quickly. He took

54

up the box and strode in under the saba. Caidrun strained after him, but Rufina gathered her up, and, smothering her with kisses, took her to get some berry cake.

"Such a bright child," Mother Turner remarked to Bennoc standing by.

"Maybe too bright for her own good," Bennoc answered soberly. "There's a reason why children don't take to heynim afore they're old and wise enough."

There was? Tamborel stared at the man. He couldn't think of one. As far as he could see, the sooner Caidy could snag heynim, the sooner she'd show how special she was. Did Bennoc sense this already? Did he guess that Caidy might even enter the Hon'faleyn, and become greater than he could ever be?

The dancing began, and someone struck up a song, and Tamborel went to play quoits with Meynoc and the others. The party was at its height, when Tamborel went to get a drink of berry cordial. He was turning from the table when Caidrun's laugh came from underneath. He stooped down, lifted the cloth.

Caidrun—with Silwender's box!

She shook it up at him in glee. "Oosiks, Brel."

Tamborel gazed at her, dismayed. If Rufina caught Caidrun with the box, there would be big trouble. He must retrieve it, fast. He reached out, but Caidrun snatched it back—so fast that she lost her balance, rolled, and let go the box. As it hit the ground, the lid flew up, and the golden heyn shot from under the table then rose into the air.

Horrified, Tamborel scrambled up. "Help! Caidrun's heyn is loose!" he yelled. The sphere was almost out of sight.

In the sudden quiet, Tamborel glimpsed upturned, startled faces. Then the heyn checked. Who had snagged it? He'd soon find out.

The little sphere descended, gaining speed. Too much speed, thought Tamborel uneasily. Someone cried out. He saw with a shock that other heynim had left their owners' clusters and were headed for Caidrun, now on her feet beside him, smiling up!

Such power! thought Tamborel. And he saw in a flash the wisdom of Bennoc's words. The power was deadly, for Caidrun lacked control. Those things were just about to hit like slingshot! Tamborel pushed her down and threw himself atop her.

Pain, hot as lancing needles struck his back, his face, his head as heynim rained down. He heard a shout, his name, and everyone went far away. . . .

•7•

Tamborel lay on his back, gazing into darkness. From high above, heynim drifted down like tiny golden bubbles, their delicate notes filling the space around him. A dream? If so, he didn't want to lose it, didn't want to awaken yet. He loosed a long, contented sigh, and, attuned to the tinkling, tumbling notes, started to drift deeper...deeper....

The notes receded. This was no dream, then. The chimes were real:

A faleyn!

Tamborel struggled back up into wakefulness, toward the harmonies. As they grew stronger, his mind cleared. Not one faleyn: two. Yornwey's, mixed in with another—not Bennoc's, not Throm's, yet he recognized it, vaguely.

He frowned, trying to remember. Whose was it, where had he heard it?

Eleyna's voice cut across his thought, shocking in its nearness. "He moved. He's coming back."

"I told you there had been a shift." That, a man speaking.

The twin faleyn twirled faster, whipping him awake. Tamborel opened his eyes. The shutters were pulled up; his chamber was flooded with light. Too bright, too bright! He squeezed up his eyes, blinded by the brilliance.

"Oh, he hurts. Do something!" Eleyna again. The shutter rattled and the brightness dimmed. His mother had sounded agitated.

Tamborel opened his eyes.

Eleyna was leaning down with such an anxious face that Tamborel hastened to reassure her. "I'm fine, Mamma." His voice was strangely raspy. Tamborel licked his lips, found them split and dry. His mouth tasted bad, his throat stuck, and he could scarcely swallow.

Water splashed into a cup. "Here, my boy." *Hwyllum?*

"Pappa!" Still at home in broad daylight? Tamborel tried to sit up. "What time is it?"

Hwyllum made to push him back, but another stopped him. "It is well: help the boy up." Yornwey.

Hwyllum raised Tamborel and propped him back against the pillows. Now he could see the healer, and the man beside her. "Casinder?" The zjarn from Pridicum. Of course! It was two years since the man's visit, but Tamborel would not forget those chimes. He gazed up at the twin heyn clusters whirling slowly now around his cot. What was everybody doing here? And why was he in bed? The touch of cool cup to his lips drove the question from his mind. He drank long, gulping drafts, so greedily that he ended in a fit of coughing, spilling water down his front. He pushed away the cup and closed his eyes. Why did he feel so weak? He began to feel frightened. "What's wrong?"

Eleyna wiped his brow. "Nothing—now. Is that not right, Yornwey?"

"You speak true, Eleyna," Yornwey agreed. "Your boy is back to stay."

Tamborel looked at her. *Back to stay?* He hadn't been anywhere.

Casinder spoke. "I shall go. One faleyn will do it now. But keep his shutter closed, Eleyna. He'll need to take light slowly, after so long."

"Yornwey, Casinder," Hwyllum said. "We can never thank you enough for returning our son. He could not have made it alone."

"Oh, I don't know," Casinder answered. "He's a stubborn one. You should be proud of him."

"Oh, we are," Hwyllum declared fervently.

"Hush," Yornwey warned. "His eyes are closed. Let

us not disturb him." The voices faded, and the chimes. Tamborel lay, wanting to call them back, but unable even to reopen his eyes. They said he'd been away. But where? Meynoc boasted of a really big escapade, once. He'd stayed out all night, he said, and hurt his leg falling from a tree. But he, Tamborel, would never do such a thing—would he? He shook his head, trying to recall.

The next day, Eleyna let Tamborel up, but not out of his room. "You've slept for days, your legs are weak. But you'll pick up again in no time."

"Slept? For *days*?" Tamborel had never heard of such a thing.

"You ... had an accident, Tam'shu."

"Accident?"

"You don't remember still?" Eleyna was eyeing him closely. "Anything—or anyone?"

"No, no. What happened?"

"I can't say now."

"But *why*?" Tamborel persisted. "It was my accident, Mamma."

"No one may speak of it at this time. Look on the bright side: you'll be out the house and through the gate before you know it."

But she didn't let him out for a full week more— and then only to go with her to the well. As he passed, everybody stared. "Mamma, why do they all look at me?"

Eleyna put her arm around him. "They're glad to see you better. See, Mistress Bider hails you. Wave back, Tam'shu."

"But why?" He'd never had such attention, even after the moldy fever.

Eleyna's arm tightened about his shoulders. "Here, you've gone quite pale. Do you want to stop and rest?"

Tamborel shook his head. He wanted to turn back home, away from all those eyes. Or, better still, find someone who would tell him what this was all about. He wriggled free. "Can I go look for Meynoc? Say yes, Mamma."

Eleyna shook her head. "You heard what Yornwey said."

"But I—"

"Nay." Eleyna's voice went sharp. "There'll be no more argument today. Now, here's the well. You want to help let down the pail?"

There came a distant shout: Meynoc with the other boys, standing by his house. "Meynoc!" The boys fell silent. Meynoc waved, and started toward him. But then the next minute, for no reason Tamborel could see, he turned tail and ran inside his gate, the others at his heels.

Tamborel watched him go, dismayed. "Why did Meynoc run from me, Mamma?"

Eleyna, intent upon the pail, did not turn around. "Rufina must have called him in, Tam'shu." The pail clanked against the well side, hit the bottom with a splash. Now she turned to him, her face concerned. "Oh dear. You look ashen. Sit, there's a good boy, and I'll turn the wheel by myself."

Tamborel perched obediently on the well sill while Eleyna cranked up the brimming bucket. He'd made no mistake. Meynoc had seen him, had come toward him, then had run as if avoiding him. And even Eleyna would not say why.

As she unhooked the loaded pail and set it down beside him, Mistress Bider bustled up, swinging an empty one. "Good day, Eleyna," she said, as though they'd never just passed in the street. "How are we, Tamborel?"

"He's much better, thank you, Mistress Bider," Eleyna said quickly.

The woman looked him over. "The scars don't show. You must be glad."

"*Please!*" Eleyna seized up the bucket, slopping water all over. "Come, Tam'shu." She took his arm and hustled him away, her heynim bobbing wildly.

Tamborel stumbled along beside her, much confused. He put a hand to his cheek. "What did Mistress Bider mean, *scars*?"

Eleyna scowled. "Not now, Tam'shu," she answered, her tone so sharp that Tamborel dared not press her further.

That night, after dinner, Hwyllum announced that he and Eleyna were off to a plenary assembly.

"A *plenary assembly*? Why, Pappa? What for?" Plenary assemblies were routine public meetings, held twice yearly in the Farmer's Hall to set sowing and harvest dates, and also seed and grain prices. So this extra assembly, coming in between, was for another reason—and an exceptional one to bring out the entire village at the height of the harvest when folk kept early nights!

"Never you mind, my boy," Hwyllum said. They put him to bed, stood over him, looking down severely. "Now be good, Tam'shu," Eleyna cautioned. "And don't leave the house," warned Hwyllum.

"Yes, Mamma; no, Pappa." Tamborel looked from one to the other. Something was up, but no use asking what. The moment they were out, Tamborel was at his saraba, peering through the slats. It wasn't easy, his saraba affording only a slice of street between houses. But he did glimpse his parents as they passed, joining other folk headed for the Farmer's Hall.

This extraordinary meeting... could it be because of him? Half a summer lost! It was as if he'd fallen into a shadow pit. Since the day of his awaking, everyone had acted strangely toward him, even Hwyllum and Eleyna. He put his hands to the sides of his head and pressed. Oh, if he could only recall...

Wincing, Tamborel removed his hands. The left side of his head felt tender. He poked about gingerly, found a sore spot in the hollow just behind his temple. He rubbed the spot, and found a patch of stubble.

Mystified, Tamborel ran into his parents' bedchamber and stood before the mirror. Reaching up on tiptoe, he turned his head sideways then with his free hand, he parted his locks, craning this way and that.

Tamborel cried out. Over the tender spot, his hair was little more than fuzz. Why, someone had shaved his scalp! He let go his curls, smoothing them into place. Couldn't see the patch now; wouldn't know it was there.

He felt around the rest of his skull and located two more such spots, one up near the crown, the second at the nape.

Three sore places on his skull! Tamborel pulled absently at the fine hair tufts, remembering Mistress Bider. *The scars don't show. You must be glad.* Eleyna had been so angry. She hadn't wanted Tamborel to hear about the scars. Why not? Tamborel could understand Hwyllum's silence, for that was Pappa's way. But Eleyna? "She always tells me," he said aloud. "Even when she's not supposed to." The scars, his long sleep, the gap in his memory: everyone in Fahwyll knew why—but him. Even Meynoc and the other boys. That was why they'd dodged him that afternoon. Was it...something bad? Tamborel grew anxious, then angry. "They have no right!"

He could not, would not wait another minute to know the truth! He threw on his clothes and ran out into the street, making for the Farmer's Hall.

·8·

Reaching the Y-fork, Tamborel paused by the well to catch his breath, a mistake. With the pause came second thoughts. He was supposed to be in bed, he'd promised to be good. He glanced back toward his house, doubtfully, then peered along the left arm of the fork toward the low, dark mass of the meeting hall blocking its end. His face set. Enough. He must know the truth about his scars, and his mysterious accident—now!

He pressed on with new resolve until he reached the hall with its low, wide entrance arch and lighted sarabas to either side. There, he stopped. So many people: the whole village! He couldn't just march in.

Everyone would turn and stare, and Mamma and Pappa would be angry at his disobedience.

Tamborel went to the nearest saraba. Standing on tiptoe, he grasped the sill and leaned in toward the open shutter slats. Silver moon moths whirred in and out and hot air puffed in his face, smelling of lamp oil and sweat, and the scented sachets that women tucked inside their bodices. The place was jammed: folk leaned against the walls, fanning themselves and mopping their brows. Above their heads their clusters bobbed and jingled agitatedly over the buzz of talk. On a far dais, facing Tamborel, Bombrul and Rufina sat side by side, stiff-backed. With them—Hwyllum and Eleyna, and between the couples, Yornwey. In front of them, Bennoc stood mopping his red face. "That child could wreck us all. We must save ourselves at any cost. The good of all outweighs the ill to one." The man sounded wrought up, unlike his usual bluff and cheery self.

"Oh!" Rufina clapped a kerchief to her mouth. Bombrul leapt up angrily. "*Ill*? That is what you'd call putting out our baby's eyes and puncturing her ears? What you propose is little short of murder!"

"Speaking of murder," Bennoc snapped back, "mind why we waited so long to convene this meeting. If young Tamborel had died, yon miss would be standing here accused of that, exactly. And we'd be talking of a remedy much stronger than stopping eyes and ears."

"Why, you—" Bombrul drew back his great fist and for a moment a fight seemed certain. But then Hwyllum stood and put himself between them, whispering in Bombrul's ear, until, slowly, the man lowered himself back onto his seat. Tamborel took fresh hold on the sill, and, wedging his toes in a wall crack, pressed his nose to the shutters just as Hwyllum spoke up aloud.

"Whether Tamborel had died, or had been hurt beyond repair, how could you, Bennoc, who tune a faleyn, even think to harm a child? To destroy the sight and hearing of an innocent baby! Who knows what such an act might bring upon our heads!"

Bennoc turned on Hwyllum angrily. "That *innocent baby* almost killed your son. Unchecked, she'll do like again, unless we stop her. What I say we should do beats any other idea proposed this night."

Yornwey stood up. "Fear stirs rash words. We must view the situation calmly." She stepped between the two men, and addressed the hall. "Many of you here have thus far spoken of anger and fear at Caidrun's extraordinary command over heynim. But look at it this way: through it, she may one day attain high honor, even in the Hon'faleyn itself. If rightly nurtured, her gift could bring great credit and renown to us here in Fahwyll.

"Yet, having seen the harm that Caidrun's gift can do while she is yet too young to wield it, I agree that we must find a way to block her—"

Bombrul was back on his feet, Rufina beside him. A clamor broke out, people shouting and waving wildly toward the dais.

Tamborel lost his grip and slithered to the ground. Caidrun? He rubbed his head. If he remembered right, she was Meynoc's baby sister. What was this frightening talk about stopping her eyes and ears? He grasped the sill anew and shimmied back up the wall. Everyone was down again, except for Yornwey. "As I was saying, we must find a way to block Caidrun's sight and hearing—*but* without harming her permanently. I urge you again: think of the future! Look to the day when she works great good and brings us glory!"

"So what do you propose, zjarn?" Bennoc demanded.

"Never mind Yornwey!" Mother Turner called out from across the hall. "Let the mother speak!"

"Very well." Yornwey nodded. "Rufina?"

Rufina leaned forward in her seat and reached for Bombrul's hand. "I'm that upset to hear you talk of our Caidrun in such a way. . . ."

Tamborel frowned. What was she saying? She spoke so low that he could scarcely hear her. He hunched up his shoulders, leaning in as far as he could go, and pressed his ear against the shutter.

". . . I never would have thought it—though, now I recall as folk said she nearly killed me even afore she was born. Poison in the blood. But 'tweren't her fault. Don't forget, she nearly died as well, the precious little innocent."

68

"The subject is, how to keep her from doing further harm," Bennoc said.

"Easy," Rufina said. "You needn't talk of maiming. I can make her a helmet to block her ears. If she don't hear heynim, she'll not snag them."

"What about her eyes? She'd still be able to see!" someone shouted.

"True," Yornwey agreed. "So we'll add a visor for when the child goes out. As for in the house, since Caidrun worries at her parents' heynim"—the zjarn turned to Bombrul and Rufina—"she must keep to her room with the helmet on except for when she sleeps. And you must start to train her straight away not to snag. Do you agree?"

"Aye. I suppose," Bombrul conceded heavily. Rufina only nodded.

"Then go, and good luck to you. I, for one, don't envy you your task."

"Nor do I," said a woman in the back row, Tamborel heard her distinctly. "Such trouble as the child is going to be. 'Twere better she had died."

Everybody stood. The meeting was over. Stunned, Tamborel slid to the ground. What was all this dreadful talk about Meynoc's baby sister? Whatever had she done? As folk streamed out into the night, Tamborel pushed his way in and hurried to the dais. Eleyna was standing with her arms about Rufina when she saw him. "Tamborel!"

"I found sore places! Here, here, and here." He

touched his fingers to the three bald spots in turn, rubbing his fingertips around, feeling the prickly stubble. "Are these the scars Mistress Bider meant?"

"Young man," Hwyllum said severely. "Did we not expressly tell you to stay abed? Did you not say that we could trust you?"

"That was before," Tamborel said.

"Please, Pappa." Eleyna crouched, taking Tamborel's hands in hers. "Yes, they're the scars, Tam'shu. We couldn't say before tonight because others are concerned."

"Caidy, you mean?"

"Caidrun? You've remembered her?"

Tamborel shook his head. "I heard through the saraba."

"Heard what? What did you hear?" Eleyna asked sharply.

Tamborel didn't answer, frightened by her tone. He thought back to the last time he'd seen the baby. Was it at her naming? Ye...es, vaguely, come to think. He'd held her heyn box. He frowned, something else picking at his mind's edge. That naming was a year ago. "I—I missed Caidy's anniversary."

"No, Tam'shu. You were there." Eleyna looked at him gravely, then to Rufina and Bombrul. "In fact, that's where you had your, your accident."

"It were no accident." Bombrul spoke up. "But for you, our Caidrun would be dead, or badly hurt, at least. You saved her, lad, just as your pappa saved her before. You are a hero, just like him."

"I am?" Tamborel stared. "But what did I do?"

Bombrul explained how Caidrun had found the heyn box, how the heyn had escaped, how she had pulled not only that one to her, but others, from every direction. "There she was, snagging heynim like slingshot. You were so quick; you saw the danger, while we stood stiff as scarecrows. You pushed her down and threw yourself atop her—"

"And the heynim struck you." Eleyna touched his scalp tenderly. "Your face was all banged up. But the back of your head took the brunt of them. Your scalp was all laid open and losing so much blood—"

"Eleyna," Hwyllum warned.

"Yornwey had to shave off your beautiful curls to stitch you up. But you wouldn't awaken for one whole week. You know the rest, Tam'shu."

"What about Caidy? Was she hurt, too?"

Eleyna shook her head. "No, Tam'shu. You shielded her."

Tamborel shuddered, recalling the talk at the meeting. That Bennoc! Ugly man! He had a sudden memory of Caidrun looking up at him from her pen, and him shaking the heyn box by her ear. She had known it at once, he remembered the joy in her big, blue eyes. "Caidy is so very special. How could Bennoc want her deaf and blind!" Tamborel clenched his fists. "I always thought he was so good and grand,

71

tuning his faleyn to the skies at sowing and harvest. I'll never like him now, never!" He turned on Rufina. "Will you really keep Caidy shut away like that?"

Rufina nodded slowly. "We must, Tamborel."

"But you can't! She must hear chiming while she's growing, or you'll cripple her anyway!"

"That does it!" Hwyllum grabbed Tamborel's shoulder and began to march him away. Rufina called them back.

"Wait! He's right." She moved forward, taking Tamborel by the hand. "It's not forever. She'll not suffer much, I promise you."

Tamborel pulled free, stepping away. The baby's own mother—did she not realize? Why, Caidy might never get back what she lost!

Hwyllum moved in. "On our way, then. Good night, Rufina. Till the morning, Bombrul," he said, and marched Tamborel away.

They passed under the hall saba, emerging into the cool night. "Try to understand, my boy: Caidrun has to be protected from herself."

"But, Pappa, Bennoc wanted to actually blind and deafen her for real!"

"You think we'd have allowed it, your Mamma, Rufina, Bombrul, Cerie, Yornwey, and I?"

"But why—"

"People were afraid. They had to vent their feelings."

"But how long must she be shut off like that, Pappa?"

72

"Until she is old enough to know better."

"But that could be *years*!" *'Twere better she had died.* . . .

Hwyllum checked his stride. "You think Rufina and Bombrul do not know this? That they don't care? And I, Caidrun's father-mentor? She's like a daughter to me. But you're my true child, my son, my own flesh and blood, and dearer to me by far. She nearly killed you, Tamborel." His voice dried up.

"She didn't mean to, Pappa."

"Of course not. But for one whole week you lay near dead because of what she did. Can you imagine what your Mamma and I went through, watching by your bed? Oh, the blood, and those terrible gashes, and Yornwey sewing you up like a flour sack!" Hwyllum seized Tamborel and hugged him, hard. Then, as suddenly, he released him, gave him a little push. "Hark at me: you have me going on like your mamma! Come on, let's get you off to bed!"

·9·

Next morning, Tamborel ran into the kitchen. "Mamma, I know what to do. You must take Caidy to Silwender!"

Eleyna pointed to the breakfast table. "Sit you down, Tam'shu."

"He'll fix her," Tamborel went on in a rush. "He must: it was all his doing in the first place."

"Oh?" Eleyna set a bowl before him.

"She felt his power before she was born. That's what started it."

"Well, we don't know that," Eleyna said. "But there was talk last night of sending for the High Zjarn." She shook her head. "We can't, though. Not right now, anyway."

"But *why*?"

"The cost, Tam'shu."

Cost? "Mamma, I don't understand."

Eleyna propped her elbows on the table. "Silwender's fee is high—too high for ordinary folk like us. Every family in Fahwyll dipped deep into its purse to meet his last one."

"You mean—the zjarns take *money*?"

"But of course."

"Yornwey too?"

Eleyna nodded. "How else would she live, but by her work, just as we live by growing grain? Zjarns cost, Tam'shu. And better zjarns cost more."

Tamborel cast around for straws. "He might fix Caidy for less—or for nothing, once we explain. He'll surely remember her. He sent her the heyn."

"My thinking exactly," Eleyna replied. "I said, `Take Caidrun to Minavar and trust to luck.' But Bombrul and Rufina were afraid, and many spoke against it. Even Yornwey said it might be wise to wait a year or two."

"A year or two!" Tamborel banged down his spoon. "Caidy mustn't be without the chimes *one day*, can't they see that?" He jumped up and made for the saba.

"Tam'shu! Where are you going?" Eleyna demanded sharply.

"To Rufina's!"

"Just you come back here!" Eleyna cried. "You go nowhere today."

"But I must—"

"That is my last word."

Tamborel stayed in that day, and for the week
thereafter. Because he was not yet quite recovered,
Eleyna said. But it was really on account of his having gone to the assembly, and also to keep him from
Rufina's until things settled down, he was sure. Each
day, he hung around the saba, gazing out, thinking of
Caidrun, wondering if the hateful helmet was yet
made, and if she wore it already. Tamborel tried to
picture how it felt, how she would get around with it
on. He covered his ears, and at once the jingle of
Eleyna's heynim was gone to a wash of toneless buzz.
He squeezed his eyes shut, and at once the world
turned dark. Keeping his eyes closed, he groped his
way around the house, bumping into furniture and
banging his head. *Poor Caidy.*

All that week, Tamborel pleaded to be let out, but
Eleyna stayed firm. Resigned, he helped with the
summertime fight against the grit that blew in under
the entrance arch and through the saraba slats. He
made his bed, dried dishes, washed vegetables, and
kept the broth pot stirred.

On the sixth day, Eleyna went to market, leaving
Tamborel behind. "Why can't I go with you?" he
protested, knowing the answer really. He recalled her
distress at the well, her dragging him home, spilling
water all the way.

She was not gone long.

"Did you see Rufina? Has Caidy got that horrible helmet yet?" he called, the moment Eleyna turned onto the front path.

"I do not know, Tam'shu." Eleyna set her basket on the kitchen table. "I did not see Rufina, I haven't seen her since the village meeting. And I spoke to no one else."

In the afternoon, Tamborel played table stones with Eleyna, he throwing the highest score. Then they drew guessing puzzles in the sand tray. With the pointed stick, Tamborel drew a circle slashed horizontally. Under the slash, he made a small, round dot.

"I give up, you win this one, Tam'shu," Eleyna conceded. "What is it?"

"Caidy's face with the helmet on," he said, erasing the lines with savage strokes. He pictured Caidrun alone in the dark. How could they bear to do it? he wondered. And to a baby who couldn't possibly understand! "I'd cry and yell until I was so sick they'd have to let me out!" The moment he was free, he'd run to Rufina's house and visit with Caidy: why not? Unlike the grownups, he had no heyn for her to snag!

But on his first day out, Eleyna took him to watch Bennoc and Throm tune their faleyn to the harvesting.

The whole village was gathered there, lining the margins of the fields, straggling all the way back to the meadow where the dead folk lay. The men, who

77

had been there since sunup, left their labors to join their families. Tamborel shaded his eyes, searching for Bombrul and Rufina. There, way over, out of reach. Meynoc stood beside them, no sign of Caidrun, of course. They had left her home, locked up.

Eleyna took his hand. "There's your pappa coming toward us. Wave to him, Tamborel. And, look, Throm and Bennoc are ready to begin."

Trailing their heynim clusters, the two men entered the fields and began to circle them in opposite directions. Even at a distance, Tamborel could hear the twin faleyn plainly, and "see" their colors with his inner eye. He looked with loathing to where Bennoc tuned his harmonies for fair skies. Last year, he'd thought the man's faleyn so wondrous, had longed to be grown-up and in his shoes. But now those harmonies sounded thin and weak. Weak sound, weak sky, thought Tamborel. He would himself have tuned the faleyn to a deeper blue; the clear, true blue of afternoon—the color of Caidy's eyes. "Bennoc's faleyn is shallow," Tamborel muttered. "So is he. Just wait till I am old enough to snag. I'll show him what a sky faleyn should sound like."

"Look, Tam'shu: now Throm draws near," Eleyna said. "See how he walks counter to Bennoc, to keep their faleyn distinct?"

Throm's faleyn, tuned to ripen the grain, was golden with a tinge of brass. Tamborel closed his eyes, and, tuning out the brass, focused on the gold, savoring the minute shift of intervals as the melodies progressed. . . . In the faleyn's spell, he saw bright, golden grain ears waving in the warm wind soft as Eleyna's long, fine hair. Sweet, plump seed to replenish the silos—and the village coffers. Last year, at harvesting, Tamborel had come into the fields with Meynoc and the rest when the men were gone. They'd played hide-and-go-seek, then stuffed themselves with fistfuls of fat grain until they were sick, although it was forbidden to touch it. He stood now, almost tasting hard, dry seed case in his mouth and moist sap sugary as nectar bursting on his tongue. . . .

"It is over, Tam'shu. Come."

Tamborel opened his eyes, coming back into the present. The people were already moving back home between the fields, talking and glancing to the clear blue skies. He let out a long, deep sigh.

Eleyna took his hand. "You're not tired? You didn't get too much sun?" Tamborel shook his head. Eleyna smiled up at Hwyllum. "It was wonderful, wasn't it, Pappa? Every year's the same!"

Tamborel walked on between his parents, saying nothing. The spell was broken. Every year was not the same. This year there was Caidy, shut away, as good as blind and deaf. Tomorrow, he resolved, he'd go to Rufina's house, whatever Eleyna said!

•10•

The very next day Eleyna took Tamborel to Rufina's house herself. Rufina looked tired and harassed. "Caidrun's taking a nap."

"Then may we wait? We came especially to see her," Eleyna said.

Rufina looked cheered. "Oh, please. She should be waking shortly."

"You look tired, Rufina."

Rufina nodded. "She's so fretful, I haven't had a moment to myself. And no one's been by, until you." The women went into the kitchen.

Tamborel went along to Caidrun's room, but he could not see inside. The archway lattice was gone and in its place, a monsoon shutter. Used only to seal outer sabas in the rainy season, the things were so thick and solid that they blocked the sound of wind and rain at the height of any storm. Tamborel put his ear to the shutter and, naturally, heard nothing. He wandered to the kitchen, where the women were seated at the table. Rufina was crying, Eleyna's arm around her shoulder. "There, now, it's not your fault, Rufina."

"But she's taking it so hard," Rufina sobbed. "Such a happy little soul as she used to be. Now all she does is cry—and the tantrums!" Rufina's heynim jiggled up and down.

Tamborel looked from one to the other. Their fault, couldn't they see? If it weren't for them, Caidrun would not have to suffer.

"I'd do anything to let her run around the house," Rufina went on.

"You can, and I know how," Tamborel declared.

"Hush, Tam'shu," Eleyna said. "Go play outside."

"But, Mamma, I do!" Tamborel looked from one to the other earnestly. "You just stow your heynim when Caidy's by. And when folk visit—they can stow their heynim, too."

"Stow heynim?" Rufina looked doubtful. "But no one has ever . . ."

"In boxes," Tamborel went on doggedly. "Like Caidy's, only bigger."

Rufina turned to Eleyna. "What do you think?"

Eleyna nodded slowly. "It's . . . worth a try." Rufina

took up the thought. "We'd have to make changes—big ones. We'd have to seal the house. It will be dark in here, and hot, and stuffy, and such a change from being open to the summer, but if there's a chance our Caidrun would be happier...I'll talk to Bombrul tonight." For an hour more, Eleyna and Rufina sat, talking over plans to change the house, no sign of Caidrun. Then it was time to go.

"But I want to see Caidy!"

"Tomorrow, Tam'shu, all right?" Eleyna said, though in the end she did not let him visit for four days after. Bombrul was enclosing his saba with a lean-to porch, working in the evenings with Hwyllum and other volunteers.

A closed-in entrance arch! It was the talk of the village! Five days later, when the work was done, Eleyna took Tamborel on a second visit.

At the sight of the porch, they came to a halt. The tiny lean-to stuck out from the house bizarrely; a narrow box with sloping roof, sealed flush with a heavy monsoon shutter. On either side, and all around the house, the sarabas were sealed also with heavy storm shields. All this, thought Tamborel, when all they had to do was take Caidy to Silwender!

Eleyna banged on the iron shutter. As they waited for Rufina to come, she shifted her feet, looking discomfited. Tamborel eyed her sideways, wondering why. After a few minutes, Rufina hauled the heavy shutter aside and let them in. At first, Tamborel could see nothing. But as he adjusted to the gloom, he saw that behind Rufina the regular saba lattice was still in place, closing off the porch from the house, turning the area into a tiny vestibule. Beyond the lattice, the middle-room was lit with lamps, just as in the monsoon season. Hard to believe it was noon, thought Tamborel. And the height of summer. He watched Eleyna pluck her heynim down and set them carefully in a box, seeing now the reason for her unease.

Inside, the monsoon-like hush gave way to eerie silence.

Tamborel looked around uneasily. It felt odd, and not very pleasant, without the heynim's jingle. And the women looked strangely bereft without their clusters.

Rufina went to fetch Caidrun. Tamborel waited by the middle room archway, watching for her to come up the passage.

Eleyna called out behind him. "Do you remember playing with her before? Is it coming back, Tam'shu?"

Tamborel nodded slowly, staring up the passageway past Rufina's bedroom arch to Caidrun's chamber at the end. "Some, Mamma. I remember the two of us chasing up and down this passageway. And Caidy cuddling a doll. And—" Something about a heyn. "And Caidy's heyn in a little box." He'd done something bad with it, though he couldn't quite remember what.

Rufina emerged, Caidrun in her arms. At the sight of Caidrun's face, Tamborel drew in his breath. Oh, the pallor of her cheeks! The dark and puffy smudges underneath her blue eyes! Not a baby's face at all!

He reached out toward her. "Caidy. You've grown."

Caidrun turned her face away, burrowing into Rufina's shoulder. He moved around to face her. "Caidy—it's me, Brel." To his horror, she began to cry. Tamborel turned to Eleyna in distress. "She doesn't know me." That hurt. For although he'd forgotten times they'd shared, his feeling for Caidrun herself was strong and clear as ever.

"She knows you, Tam'shu. All too well."

"How do you mean, Mamma?"

Rufina walked Caidrun about the room, jigging her up and down, stroking her head, and soothing her ear with gentle words.

"You mean the accident? You told me she wasn't hurt."

"She wasn't, *bodily*. But she got a bad fright. There was quite a to-do after you went down: shouting and goings-on. Give her time."

"Let go! Let go!" Caidrun kicked and struggled to be set down.

"Ignore her, Tamborel," Rufina advised, setting Caidrun to the floor. "Let her come to you."

Freed, Caidrun ran around the room, picking up things and hurling them aside, cutting a swath.

"She seems to have gotten out on the wrong side," Eleyna said lightly.

"That's normal these days," Rufina answered. "All we've done to make life easier is still not enough. She misses the sunlight."

And the *chimes*, thought Tamborel. He missed

them, too, even after this short while. The total absence of familiar, reassuring sound made him feel most uneasy, even anxious. He well remembered how much they'd meant to Caidrun. She must be going crazy!

Caidrun went to the saba lattice and rattled it, still ignoring her visitors. "Out! Out!" she commanded.

"I'll take her," Tamborel volunteered quickly. "In the baby cart."

Rufina shook her head. "Not today, Tamborel."

"Tomorrow, then? I'd wheel her to the brook. That's well clear of the fields. And Meynoc could come, too. Please, Rufina?"

"Oh, Tamborel. You're such a kind boy. But you're way too young to take her alone. Even with Meynoc."

Tamborel drew himself up. "I'm nearly eight."

"I'll go with him," Eleyna said quickly, then glanced upward. "I—I'll leave my heynim home. Won't hurt, I suppose, just for a short while."

Rufina beamed. "You'd do that? We'll all go, then. Caidrun can wear her helmet, and we'll take it off once she's out of harm's way." She gathered Caidrun up and smothered her with kisses. "Oh, my dearest little one— we'll make you happy somehow, wait and see!"

Around noon the next day, Eleyna filled a picnic basket for their outing. Then, stowing her heynim in a box, she set it on the mantel shelf. At the saba, she hesitated, looking most unhappy.

"You don't have to leave them behind altogether, Mamma. Bring them in the basket."

"But Caidrun will hear them when she takes her helmet off, Tam'shu."

"Not if you leave your box in Rufina's porch."

"But it hardly seems worth it, for just that little way." Nevertheless, Eleyna ran back, took down the box and slipped it inside the basket. "Let's go." At last, the two of them stepped out into the street.

Mistress Bider was at her gate, little Tancey peeping from behind. She stared at the space above Eleyna's head. "Well, I never!"

"Going to Rufina's, are you?" Mother Turner came out to meet them. "Good for you. How is the little one?"

Tamborel strode ahead impatiently. When he reached Rufina's, Caidrun was waiting by the saba lattice. "Brel!" The moment the lattice was open, she grabbed his sleeve and towed him inside. Just like the old days, thought Tamborel, his spirits lifting. She'd come around to him at last!

"Come, Caidrun. We're going on a picnic!" Rufina scooped Caidrun up.

Caidrun scowled. "No," she said. "No, no, no."

The helmet was made of the coarse brown stuff the men wore in the fields, and thickly padded. There were two earflaps buttoned back, and a rolled up visor. As Rufina tried to slip it on, Caidrun kicked and fought, squalling loudly. The helmet covered her brow and half her cheeks, also. As Rufina tied the drawstring knots, Caidrun struggled. "Off! Off!"

Rufina pressed on grimly, fastening the earflaps under Caidrun's chin. Then she rolled down the visor, covering the wide blue eyes.

"You can't do that!" Tamborel cried. "It's cruel!"

"Only till we're away from everyone," Rufina called loudly over Caidrun's protests. "Let's go, quick!" They set out, along the street. Rufina carried Caidrun in her arms, Tamborel pushed the empty baby cart, while Eleyna toted the loaded basket. People stared as they hurried along, but no one spoke to them. Propelled by Caidrun's squalling, they hurried to the end of the street, and away from the fields to the brook.

There, Eleyna spread out the picnic things while Rufina removed the helmet. Caidrun stopped her racket instantly, and, blinking in the bright sunshine, ran to the edge of the brook, looking down.

"Watch her, Tamborel," Eleyna called.

Not that there was much danger, for the brook was only inches deep there, rippling over smooth, round stones. Minnows started at Caidrun's shadow, making her squeal, this time with delight.

Tamborel picked up a pebble and threw it into the water, scattering quicksilver needles. Catching the dart of the fish, Caidrun jumped up and down, laughing and clapping her hands. Tamborel handed her a pebble. "Here, Caidy. You throw one, too."

Caidrun stretched out her arm and the pebble plopped into the current. " 'Gain, Brel! 'Gain!" she cried. Her cheeks were flushed, her clear blue eyes bright with excitement. Tamborel sighed with satisfaction.

They had to come again. Perhaps if he waited, picked his moment, they might let him bring Caidrun here tomorrow after all. . . .

·11·

After that, Rufina and Eleyna took Caidrun out as often as Tamborel could persuade them. "She's more like her old self again, Tamborel. And so glad to be about, she doesn't seem to mind the helmet as much," Rufina said.

Eleyna was not so satisfied. "All these walks and picnics: the house is getting into such a sorry state. I wish Rufina would go out on her own." But she would not brave the stares and comments without Eleyna.

"I could take Caidy out alone," Tamborel suggested. "I know what to do. Ask Rufina, *please*?"

They sent him on a trial trip, wheeling Caidrun

nonstop to the brook and back—a safe enough outing through fallow meadow. He pushed her in little spurts, then pulling up, making Caidrun squeal and beg for more. Then he rushed her back at breakneck speed to keep her mind off her helmet. After a few more such trips, Rufina showed him how to knot and unknot the helmet laces. Then came the biggest test of all.

Rufina set Caidrun before him. "Tamborel's fitting your helmet today. If you let him, he'll wheel you to the brook. He'll take it off there and put it back on when it's time to come home." She handed the helmet to Tamborel.

"Here. See what she does."

With trembling fingers, Tamborel set the thing on Caidrun's head. Please, he prayed. Don't fuss, Caidy. To his relief and Rufina's amazement, Caidrun suffered him to close the flaps and knot the strings the way he'd been shown. She clung to him without demur as he carried her out and set her in the baby cart.

They were off. As usual, Tamborel ran, bumping over ruts and stones. There, he carefully undid the knots and—oh, the look on her face as he raised the helmet and uncovered her eyes! She stood up, blinking, in the cart and threw her arms about him. "Brel!" she cried, and they both laughed aloud.

He jumped her down and they went splashing in the stony shallows until they were both drenched.

Then they chased up and down the bank while the shadows lengthened into late afternoon. At last, Tamborel led her back to the cart. Now, he thought, tensing up, the final test. He held up the helmet. "Time to put it back on, Caidy. But we'll come again tomorrow, promise."

Caidrun sat, unprotesting, while he slipped the helmet back on and tied the straps. She knows, he thought exultantly. No reason they shouldn't go out every day now!

Afternoons from then on, he wheeled Caidrun to the brook. He threw stones—actually managed to skim one—and delighted to see her eyes light up, to hear her laugh when the pebble bounced. "You're so kind," Rufina said. "And steady, coming day in, day out to give our Caidrun an airing. If only our Meynoc would do half as much!"

Eleyna was not so glad. "Spend so much time with a two-year-old baby? It's not natural. You're not her family, Tam'shu."

"But I am, Mamma, in a way."

"And you've done nothing else for a week, things you love to do, like fishing. I'm going to have to speak with your pappa."

That night, Tamborel lay listening to their murmur. About him, he knew. And it was not good, judging by their serious tone. He went off to sleep, full of misgiving. Next morning, when Tamborel went to breakfast, Hwyllum was still there. "Eat up, my boy. You're going to the field today."

"But, Pappa! I promised to take Caidy to the brook."

Hwyllum shook his head. "Not this day, Tamborel. And not tomorrow, either. You're seeing too much of that lass."

"I *must* take her. She counts on me! Who else will wheel her out?"

"Rufina. It's her place," Hwyllum said firmly. "We're doing more than our fair share."

"No, we're not, Pappa. You're Caidy's second father, and that makes me her second brother. We should help her more than others do."

Hwyllum's face darkened. "Are you saying I don't care?" He went on, softening his voice. "Listen, your mamma's right: you should be out doing boyish things, not wheeling out a baby girl."

"But I *like* to be with Caidy. We have fun together!" Tamborel met his father's eyes, read the steely purpose there, and quailed. Still, he tried again. "Let me go just today, please, Pappa. I'll come with you tomorrow."

"No, Tamborel. You'll see Caidrun next week. Now eat and get dressed."

"But Rufina—"

"We'll tell Rufina on the way to work."

"*You* tell her!" Tamborel cried, beside himself. "I'm staying home!" He ran to his room and sank onto his bed. To have spoken to one's father so! He heard

92

Hwyllum leave, Eleyna set about her housework. He waited, but she didn't call on him to help, she didn't come near him at all. Tamborel pictured Caidrun, awaiting his knock. She'll never understand, he thought grimly. She'll think that I've abandoned her.

Tamborel kept to himself all that day, and the next, sitting in silence at table, scarcely touching his food, and avoiding his parents' eyes. But if they cared, they did not show it. Neither did they relent.

After five days, Tamborel could stand it no longer. Hwyllum and Eleyna really meant what they said this time, it was clear. So the sooner he came around, the sooner they'd let him visit Caidrun. The next day, Hwyllum took him to the fields. One week after that, Tamborel stood before Rufina's porch.

Rufina let him in gladly. "Caidrun's not well. She misses you."

Tamborel took heart. Caidy will welcome me, after all, he thought. But when she saw him, she scowled and turned away.

"See, Caidrun," Rufina said. "Brel's come to take you out."

Caidrun regarded them both, her eyes unsmiling. "Brel go home."

"Now, Caidrun," Rufina said. "Come, let's get your helmet on."

Caidrun fought and wriggled on Rufina's lap, resisting all attempts to fit the helmet. Rufina gave up the struggle. "You'd better go, Tamborel."

Caidrun stopped fighting instantly. "Caidy ride!" she bawled.

Rufina turned to Tamborel, at a loss. "Will you manage?"

Tamborel raced along the path, setting the little cart a-bounce, but Caidrun only clutched the cart sides grimly. At the brook, she tore at the helmet. "Off! Off!"

Tamborel undid Rufina's careful knots, releasing Caidrun's wiry mop. He scooped up a handful of stones, threw the first, then handed one to Caidrun. "Now you, Caidy," he said. She drew back her small fist and, to his consternation, hurled the stone at *him*! Of course, she let it go all wrong, and it landed by her own feet, but Tamborel was deeply hurt. "I'm sorry I didn't come, Caidy," he said. "I had to help my pappa in the fields." Casting around for some way to cheer her up, he recalled how she'd liked his singing.

"Caidy, do you remember this? 'One ear of grain, two ears of grain, three and another make four—' "

Caidrun turned away with a flourish.

He sighed, gazing at the back of her head, the stiff set of her shoulders. Oh, if only he were seventeen instead of seven: he'd share his heynim with her, even with them in a box! He had a flash of her from long ago, face upturned, demanding. *Oosiks, Brel! Oosiks!* What to do? He had no heynim to shake, but . . . He could try to sing their notes.

Tamborel began to hum, a snatch from Silwender's chiming the night he'd lain beneath Rufina's sill. He couldn't remember it exactly, but he'd not forgotten it entirely, either. It came into his mind sometimes, when he was going off to sleep. He hummed it once, softly, tentatively, then, gathering confidence, he repeated it more loudly, adjusting a couple of notes. That got Caidrun's attention, all right. She grasped his jacket and tugged. "Moosic, Brel, moosic!"

"You want more?" Tamborel smiled. "Well, let's see: here are some notes from Yornwey's cluster." Instead of humming this time, he sang out the notes in clear, bell-like *O*'s: "O, O, O, O, O, O." He smiled. "Aren't they lovely? Only Yornwey has those notes, you know. Now these are the ones in my mamma's cluster: listen." Tamborel intoned the half-dozen high, thin notes. "Of course, my singing doesn't sound a bit like chimes, but it's better than nothing, right, Caidy?"

Caidrun jumped up and down waving her arms. "More, Brel, more."

Tamborel sang more clusters, naming each one, until, tiring at last, Caidrun was off and running along the bank.

But her humor was restored.

They played on peaceably until it was time to go, but the moment Tamborel took up the helmet, Caidrun squealed and ran. Tamborel caught her, but he could not get the helmet on. "Listen," he yelled at last. "If you don't let me put this thing back on, they'll never let us out again!"

Caidrun quit her squalls abruptly, and held still while Tamborel tied on the helmet. But as he made to roll down the visor, he stopped. After all his effort, Caidrun's face was stiff and set again. Surely it wouldn't hurt to leave off the helmet until they were closer to home? He trudged along, pushing the cart before him, Caidrun facing front, fixed on the path ahead. Tamborel sighed, thinking of the dark and silent house waiting to imprison her. Poor Caidy. He resolved to sing to her every day from now on. But that was no substitute for hearing true heynim. How long, before she suffered lasting harm? He pushed on, lost in anxious thought, until suddenly, Caidrun exclaimed.

Coming toward them were several village wives, talking and not looking where they were going. Their heynim! While Caidrun might not hear, she could surely see them—and had! Tamborel ran around to cover Caidrun's eyes—too late. One of the women cried out as a pair of heynim detached from her cluster and floated toward the cart. "Caidy—*no!*" Tamborel yanked Caidrun's visor down, grabbed the cart handles and ran.

The errant heynim floated back to their owner, too late.

"There's that miss," someone called. "What's Rufina thinking of? Is that Eleyna's boy? He's far too young to mind the child. . . ."

Tamborel blundered along, leaving the women behind. His face burned, his breath came short, his blood was salty in his throat. Not true! Not true! Of all the luck! Deaf to Caidrun's squalling, he pressed on toward Rufina's. He handed Caidrun over in the porch and hurried home, not stopping to explain. The minute Hwyllum got home Tamborel was called out.

"I meant no harm. Nobody ever goes that way," he mumbled. Only Meynoc and the rest—and not even them right now, for they were helping with the harvest. As for the women, he'd never seen them at the brook before.

Eleyna and Hwyllum exchanged glances. "There," Eleyna said, putting her arm around him. "We don't blame you, eh, Pappa?"

Hwyllum nodded. "But this afternoon has stirred up more strong talk about Caidrun."

"So many have offered to help mind Caidrun now," Eleyna went on. "Yornwey, and Cerie, and Mother Turner, and Mistress Fossek—and me, of course. We're taking turns to wheel Caidrun out every day. Your pappa and Bombrul, too, when they can. So, you see, good has come of it, after all, Tam'shu." She enveloped him in a warm embrace. "And everybody says how kind you've been, helping out like that."

Tamborel could hardly speak. "Do I take turns, too?"

Eleyna looked to Hwyllum. Hwyllum nodded. "You can go to Rufina's once a week to play with Caidrun—when you're not helping me, like. And once in a while take her to the brook with Mamma and me, maybe."

Tamborel fled to his room and huddled on his bed. All those people, meddling in Caidy's life. And how would he sing to her every day now? How would he ever sing to her again with someone always listening in!

·*12*·

Harvesting came and went. Tamborel worked hard
in the fields each day with Hwyllum, hoping that
when his parents saw how he had grown, they'd relent and let things be as they were. Meantime, no
more outings to the minnow brook: he had to make
do with the weekly visit to Rufina's. There, it was like
treading prickly grain stubble barefoot. So that
Caidrun could roam free without her helmet, Rufina
stowed her heynim on the porch. This left her edgy
and quick-tongued, unlike her usual, even-tempered
self. Some days, Caidrun was also moody and difficult
and nothing could please her. Then, Tamborel wondered why he went at all. One morning, they both
turned on him together.

"Sing, Brel. Caidy want Brel to sing." Her pale face was tilted up at him, pinched, demanding.

Rufina came out of the kitchen. "You're going to sing, Tamborel?" She perched on a nearby chair. "How she loves that. Go on."

Tamborel felt the color rush to his face. "I can't sing. Not right now," he mumbled. Caidrun began to fuss.

"Please," Rufina said. "She's getting upset, Tamborel."

"Oh, well." He began the chant. "One ear of grain, two ears of grain, three and another make four—" Caidrun cut him off. "No, no, no! Brel sing *moosic*!"

Rufina turned to him, perplexed. "What does she mean, music?"

Tamborel shook his head. But he knew right enough. She wanted him to sing the heyn notes again. But he dared not, for he was sure it was wrong, somehow. Caidrun began to beat him with her fists, until Rufina pulled her off. "Just stop that, Caidrun, or you'll go to your room with your helmet on, you hear?" Caidrun's mouth clamped shut. And, oh, the look she shot him!

Tamborel couldn't stand it any longer. He decided to take a risk. After all, Rufina was Caidrun's mamma, and she seemed to understand her better than the others. "If I sing what Caidy wants," he said slowly, "you must promise not to tell."

Rufina frowned. "Tell?" She shook her head. "I

don't understand. But whatever it is, Tamborel, I promise. Go on."

Tamborel turned to Caidrun. "You want to hear your mamma's notes? Here:" He intoned Rufina's heynim in turn, four high, pure notes climbing down, four more going up again, like steps.

"Pretty! Pretty!" Caidrun clapped her hands. "'Gain, Brel! 'Gain!"

"Why," exclaimed Rufina. "They're the notes of my cluster, exactly. I don't believe it! How did you do it, Tamborel?"

Tamborel stared at her, surprised. Up until this minute, he'd assumed that everybody else could do the same. "They're in my head, that's all."

Rufina eyed him, marveling. "I never heard them laid out clear like that. They sound such a jumble to me, always overlapping. Sing them again." Tamborel obliged, this time arranging them zigzag, alternately high and low.

"Do your mamma and pappa know you can carry heynim notes like this?" Rufina asked him. Tamborel recoiled. "No, no one must know, you promised."

"I don't see why," Rufina said. "It's not as if you're using actual heynim. And it doesn't seem right, keeping such a gift quiet—from your own folk, too. Yet I'll hold my tongue," she assured him hurriedly. Scooping up Caidrun, Rufina hugged her tight. "Look at her: she's smiling!"

Tamborel sang on through the fall, but after the

monsoons set in, his singing, his very visits ceased. Now all the folk were crowded indoors, imprisoned by the driving rains. It was a trial at best. For the men whose lives were open field and sky, for the wives with families underfoot, for the children unable to go out and play. Sickness abounded, due to wet and chill and damp. Mistress Bider was kept busy dispensing decoctions for the ague and rheum; Yornwey tuned her faleyn to the fusty grain pox and moldy fever. Almost everyone succumbed to flagging spirits after long successive days of dark gray skies.

But the monsoons passed, as they always did, and spring arrived. The village threw off its monsoon shutters and emerged, blinking, under the sun to dry out. Dearly as he wished to go see Caidrun, Tamborel had to help Hwyllum every day, breaking up the soggy ground, clearing ditches. Meynoc was there, also, helping Bombrul. He had certainly shot up over the winter months, Tamborel noticed. To his father's shoulder now!

On Tamborel's first visit after the monsoons, Caidrun gave him a hard time. As if it had been his fault that he had not come. But in the end she forgave him, and things were as before. Then, suddenly, it was Caidrun's second anniversary.

It was a quiet affair, indoors, with few guests—no children, save for Meynoc and Tamborel. Eleyna, Hwyllum were invited. Cerie, and Yornwey. Mother

Turner and Mistress Fossek arrived, gathering their heynim and stowing them on the porch.

"Where's our anniversary girl?" Eleyna looked expectantly around.

"Rufina's bringing her directly," Bombrul said, and Caidrun burst upon them, swathed in bright pink flounces. The frills at sleeve and hem made her arms and legs look thin and pitifully bony, and the pink made her skin seem sallow. Her hair, which Tamborel loved to see flaring out around her head, was scraped back and caught behind each ear in huge pink bows.

Tamborel moved up. "Happy anniversary, Caidy."

Caidrun ran to him, hugging his knees. "Sing, Brel, sing!"

Tamborel felt his cheeks flare. "Not right now, Caidy."

For a moment, he feared she would burst into a squall, but instead she merely turned from him and ran to Bombrul, clamoring to be picked up.

"Never mind, Tam'shu," Eleyna murmured. "She's cranky from her nap."

Not so, Mamma, Tamborel answered silently, and braced for trouble.

"My, how you've grown, young lady," Yornwey said. "Good thing I brought you a size larger new dress. Here." Yornwey held out a parcel, brightly wrapped. Caidrun seized it and hurled it from her.

"Here, here, my girl." Bombrul set her down. "Mind your manners. Open the pretty that Yornwey has brought you." Caidrun beat her fists against Bombrul's legs, then ran to her mother. Rufina looked around at everyone, quite at a loss. "Perhaps if we ignore her . . ."

Caidrun stamped her feet and tugged Rufina's skirts. "Don't want!"

"Meynoc, hand the juice cups around," Bombrul said loudly.

"No! No! No!" Caidrun tore off a ribbon and threw that down now. Her hair, freed on one side, sprang out like frytt-burrs.

Rufina looked around apologetically. "She's not that used to company, you know?" She turned to Caidrun. "Come now, dear. Be nice."

Caidrun ran from the room. Rufina made to follow, but Bombrul pulled her back. "She'll come around. Let's get on with the party."

As soon as everyone was occupied, Tamborel fled to Caidrun's room. He found her huddled in a corner, staring at the floor. "Caidy? Want to play?"

She turned her back.

He started to sing a song. No response. He tried a heyn note or two, softly, but even that did not work. Laughter floated down the passage, the stilted sound of people ill at ease. Tamborel made a face. Why didn't they just be quiet? They only made things worse. Still . . . there they all were, standing heynless for Caidrun's sake. Then again . . . "Serve them right," he said aloud. If they'd taken Caidy to Silwender in the first place, they would not have this mess. Right now, what Caidrun needed most was to hear heynim again. Or just one—the one that was rightfully hers.

Tamborel slipped into the next room up the passage: Rufina's. No sign of the heyn box, but then they wouldn't leave it lying around these days. He poked around some more, opening closet doors and chest drawers. . . . He climbed onto the bed, craning up to the high shelf over the night table—and there it was! Tamborel reached it down. Somewhere, deep inside, the voice of caution sounded. *Bad boy. You know it's wrong. There'll be trouble.*

It's only for a moment, he told himself. To cheer her up on her anniversary. No one need ever know. So where's the harm?

Caidrun hadn't moved. Tamborel strode over, put the box to her ear, and jiggled it. Caidrun whipped around, her face transfigured. " 'Gain!"

Tamborel obeyed. Beaming, Caidrun snatched at the box and Tamborel whipped it around to her other side, just as he had long ago. And they were off, playing tag with the heyn box, all around the room. In the light of the lamps, Tamborel could see the flush on Caidrun's cheeks, and the sparkle in her eyes. Finally, she caught the box, and pulled. "Brel give Caidy!"

Tamborel shook his head. "No," he said, and tugged it free, held it out of reach. Caidrun's smile vanished.

She opened her mouth and let forth a screech. "Give Caidy, give Caidy, *give Caidy*!"

Silence in the middle room. Tamborel looked toward the arch. Any minute they would come rushing to see what was wrong. Where to hide the box? In a panic, Tamborel stuffed it down his shirt. A moment later, in they came. "What happened, Tamborel? What's wrong?"

Tamborel swallowed, trying to think up some excuse. But he needn't have bothered. The grown-ups crowded around Caidrun, all talking at once. He slipped out, restored the box, and made for the middle room just as they brought in Caidrun to open her gifts.

Now Tamborel kept his distance, watched her tear the wrapping from each present then toss both aside. Rufina tried to put her back to bed, but Caidrun would have none of it. So the grownups tried once more to ignore her, hoping that she would settle down. Tamborel eyed Caidrun guiltily. All his fault she was so out of sorts. But he'd only tried to make her happy on her anniversary.

Meynoc invited him into his room to throw table stones. Tamborel went thankfully. They had not been playing long when a row erupted outside. They ran to find Caidrun, defiant, triumphant in the porch, the empty boxes scattered at her feet. And in the air above her head? Heynim—everybody's, all mixed in together!

Part Three

•13•

"Hold up, boy, don't walk so fast. What's fired you up this soon in the day—or shouldn't I ask?"

"Sorry, Pappa." Tamborel pulled back, matching his long stride to Hwyllum's stiff, early-morning gait, ignoring the pointed jibe. It didn't take much for his father to guess that he and Caidy had quarreled again. But he couldn't afford to admit it. They passed the well, and went on, toward the fields. As they neared Caidy's house, Tamborel slowed, and now Hwyllum drew ahead. "I suppose you'll be stopping by to make up with her again?" His father glanced back, shaking his head. "That miss. I don't know why you persist. Where's your self-respect?"

Tamborel halted by Caidy's gate. "I won't be long, Pappa. I promise."

Hwyllum sighed. "Very well, Tamborel. But this is all going to stop."

Frowning, Tamborel watched Hwyllum trudge on toward the fields. The threat was not new, but the tone was sharper. He turned anxiously up the garden path. Hwyllum had never liked his friendship with Caidy, still watched for an excuse to part them, and she was no help. Always difficult, always picking fights, venting her eternal wrath on him. "One day you'll go too far," he'd warned her, just the night before. But she'd only taunted him, as usual, pushing him to walk away for good. Rufina was at the lattice. "You want Caidy? I'll see if she's up."

Tamborel unslung his hoe and rake and waited by the step. Hwyllum was already out of sight. *Too much!* Caidy knew he'd be on his way to work and in a rush. He was about to go when she appeared. "What do you want?" Judging by her tousled hair and crumpled shift, she'd come straight out of bed.

"Will you be my partner at the Harvest Gathering or not, Caidy?"

She eyed him sourly. "I will not, I told you so last night. Besides, why would you want to go with me?"

"Because—oh, please don't start again. Because we're best friends. Will you?" Her face said no. That this last bout of bickering was not yet over. Tamborel heaved a big sigh. Oh, why was he always the one to make the peace? He almost turned and walked away, until he caught the look in her eyes. She was testing him again. "Three days ago, you said you'd like it."

"That was then. Perhaps we should stop seeing each other. That's what Hwyllum wants."

That old song again? Tamborel's spirits sank. "Not true! Hwyllum's your father-mentor. He loves you."

"Not any more." She flicked a hand toward the stream of men heading for the fields. "Hwyllum doesn't even *like* me. In fact, he wishes I'd just vanish. Everybody does. But you, Brel, everybody loves you." She looked up at him archly. "You're much too good for me."

"Stop it." Tamborel glanced up the road. "Look, I have to—"

"And quite the man now. Tancey Bider fancies you."

Tamborel felt his face catch fire. "Caidy, stop this minute!"

"Your folk say you and I—our closeness—is . . . not natural. Even now, when I hardly see you any more," she added, sticking in another barb.

"Hah! That's not true."

"They've fixed for you to take Tancey to the Gathering."

"Nonsense! Listen, if I can't take you, I shan't go." He turned and ran, her shout in his ears:

"Just you wait, Brel: you'll soon see how right I am!"

All day he hoed and raked, taking it out on the soil. Time was when he always could read Caidrun's thought and gauge her mood, could sense exactly how she felt—and why. But now? She was always nursing some imagined slight or insult. *Hwyllum doesn't even like me. In fact, he wishes I'd just vanish.*

Whatever she says or does, however much she goads me, he told himself, I cannot, *will* not turn my back on her. She can't help the way she is. They've made her like this, shutting her away for so long.

"I smell rain." Hwyllum straightened, and, leaning on his hoe, took out his kerchief and mopped his brow. Grateful for the interruption, Tamborel stopped also. Clouds were massing, the air had taken on the eerie violet glow that threatened storm. Tamborel eyed his father covertly. The slow, careful moves, the wince as he looked up: Hwyllum's back was acting up again.

Lightning flashed, thunder rolled, and several neighbors shouldered tools and headed for home. To Tamborel's relief, Hwyllum followed suit.

"Your mamma and I were talking," his pappa remarked, as they crossed the field. "About the Harvest Gathering."

"Oh?" Tamborel braced himself.

"Mamma said that Tancey Bider expects you to take her."

Tamborel pulled up short. Was Caidy right, then? Had his parents—and Mistress Bider—really plotted behind his back? He let his breath out slowly. If so, could he blame them? He was nothing short of an embarrassment: going on eighteen and still unattached. Meynoc was wed, and the rest were spoken for. Worse . . . With great effort, Tamborel kept himself from glancing to the silent, vacant space above his head.

Not a day went by without his reliving that first, humiliating attempt to snag a heyn. There he was, standing in the street with Hwyllum and Eleyna, and Yornwey turning to him with a smile. "We have all the heynim we need. Shall we give Tamborel this last one?"

He'd felt so proud. At thirteen and some he was surely ready. He remembered stepping out to claim the passing sphere. With all eyes fixed on him, he'd bent his mind toward it. He well recalled the prick of elation as it checked, bounced, then began to move his way. He heard again the gasp, as, suddenly, it halted, wavered for a heartbeat, then sailed up into the blue.

Tamborel had fled home, wanting to die. Hwyllum and Eleyna had gone after him, and Yornwey.

"Don't worry, Tamborel," the zjarn said. "It's too soon, that's all."

"Too soon? I'm almost fourteen." Meynoc had held three heynim by then! "There's something wrong with me, isn't there? You saw the heyn begin to move, then stop. I swear I didn't let my mind slip, so why did I lose the thing—*why*?"

Yornwey shook her head. "As it checked, did you feel anything inside?"

Tamborel put his hands to his temples and pressed. "I . . . don't know."

"Well, no use fretting now," Yornwey said. "Next year you'll do fine."

That next year had come and gone with like result. Again, he'd snagged a heyn, then, as it had begun to lurch toward him, he'd lost it the same way. Folk talked then, for being heynless was unheard of. Some blamed his old accident; others, Caidrun, though what his affliction had to do with either, he failed to see. The fact remained that for some strange reason, he stood out in the street year after year, willing just one small sphere to bend to his command—in vain. Why? he asked himself during long, sleepless nights. Why, of all people, should he be so bereft? He had a finer sense of harmony than Yornwey, and Bennoc and Throm. So why not a greater power to snag? The two were said to go together. To think he'd once dreamed of becoming a zjarn! Of entering the Hon'faleyn and winning renown with healing harmonies. . . .

Sometimes, when Caidrun was in a rage, she taunted him with her own handful—all she was allowed, being not yet thirteen. "Poor Heynless One," she sneered, mocking him as no one else would dare. Only the night before she'd goaded him, as he'd tried to show her how to adjust a heyn's pitch.

"Spin it faster and you raise the tone; slow it down and you lower it." Caidrun wouldn't listen, didn't want to learn. "But your cluster's such a *jumble*, Caidy. You could make it so much more harmonious."

"Let me be, *Heynless Wonder*. It's my cluster. I like it as it is."

"Heynless Wonder, am I? I'd rather be that than hold your ill-tuned hodgepodge. It rattles like a can of nails. I marvel that you sleep nights!"

Tamborel clenched his fists. Not Caidy's fault that she was difficult, that she lacked a fine ear. Folk had made her this way—and now they punished her for it. He turned to face Hwyllum. "I'm not going to the feast, Pappa."

Hwyllum's face stiffened. "Not going?" Another clap of thunder came as the first large raindrops splattered down. "We'll talk of this at home," Hwyllum said curtly, moving on. "I'll not stand out here getting drenched, arguing with a disobedient son."

There came a sudden, distant shout. "Bre . . . el!"

Caidrun, running toward them, her heynim jigging discordantly.

"Now what does *she* want?" Hwyllum muttered.

Caidrun's cheeks were flushed, her blue eyes unusually bright. Her hair bushed out around her face. "I changed my mind," she said, her eyes on Hwyllum. "I'll go with you to the Harvest Gathering, after all."

Hwyllum's head snapped around. "What's that?" He craned past her to Tamborel. "You have asked Caidrun? Just now you said you would not go!"

Tamborel swallowed. "I—was mistaken."

"I'll say!" Hwyllum looked to Caidrun. "He's taking Tancey Bider."

"That I'm not!"

"Indeed you are, young man!" Hwyllum looked thunderous as the dark clouds roiling overhead.

"I've not even asked her."

"Oh, but you will, you will."

"You mean—it's already planned?" Tamborel glanced to Caidrun, and knew then that she'd provoked this scene on purpose.

Hwyllum cleared his throat. "I did say as how your mother—"

"You said Tancey Bider expected me to ask her."

"No, I did not." Hwyllum shook his head emphatically. "I said as how she expected you to *take* her, which is quite a different crock of seed."

"That it is!" Tamborel cried, beside himself. "Well, I'll not do it! How will I look, taking a girl my parents picked for me—and behind my back!"

"So Brel can be my partner, after all," Caidrun chipped in brightly. "Is that not so, father-mentor, dear?"

Hwyllum's face went deep, dark red. "A man squires a *sweetheart* to a feast, not a twelve-year-old chit. Whatever Tamborel says here and now"—his voice rose—"he's taking Mistress Bider's lass, and that's my final word."

·14·

Tamborel ate supper fast, while Hwyllum scolded and Eleyna looked on with reproachful eyes. The meal over, he ran to ask Caidrun out for an evening walk. They made for the brook, speaking little, though Tamborel could feel her eye upon him. At the water's edge, she stopped and turned about.

"So? How is it with Hwyllum?"

Scooping up a pebble, Tamborel sent it skimming. "He's furious. Even Eleyna's upset." Caidrun laughed. "Good. Serve him right. Serve them both right."

"Caidy!"

"Let's cross over, shall we?" Caidrun took off her shoes, slid down the bank and edged out into the water. "Oooh, it's deliciously cool, and—oh! Watch out, these stones have grown *so-o-o* slippery."

Tamborel swallowed his annoyance and followed. They slipped and slithered across the pebbly bed, scrambled up the other side and sat, chafing their numbed feet. Presently, they lay back, gazing up into the storm-washed sky. "So clean and bright," Caidrun murmured. "As if the clouds had polished everything."

Tamborel had to smile. Caidy and her fancies. Who else would see rain clouds as polishing rags? And yet . . . things did seem better now. The sky was clear; the light, sharp, and colors looked bright and clean. He loosed a cautious breath, unwinding, some.

There came a slight jingle from Caidrun's cluster. "I still wonder where they come from, Brel. Remember the arguments we used to have?"

Tamborel nodded. "You said they were drops from the sun."

"Hah, now I know better: heynim are not natural, but made."

"*Made*?" This was new. "How so?"

"They're metal. Metal comes from ore. And ore is worked by smiths."

"But what smiths? And where?" Tamborel shook his head. "If that were so, folk would know it."

Caidrun sat up. "Not necessarily. They say the world is a big place."

Tamborel smiled up at her. "Caidy, why do you persist?"

118

"Why?" Caidrun plucked down a heyn and handed it across. "Here, take it. Shake it in your fist." Tamborel enclosed the little sphere hesitantly in his palm. So long, since he'd held one . . . He shook it, felt faint vibrations—and something shift within.

"Well?" Caidrun demanded, as he handed it back. "Admit it, Brel." She released it to rejoin her cluster. "The heyn is hollow and something's loose in there, causing it to chime."

"No one would dispute that, Caidy."

"Then no one would dispute that they are made."

"There are other natural things just like this that we can't explain."

"Such as?"

"Such as frytt-burrs." At harvest, the spiny frytt-burrs burst amid the grain, letting out their delicate, translucent treasure: small white globes that rose above the fields like ghostly heynim. Each contained small brown seeds, embarking on a perilous bid for life. *Fools' heynim*, folk called them. "Then there's the colly bean," Tamborel went on. Too sour for cooking, each oval bean encased a grub, which ate its way out, emerging as a silver moon moth. "The frytt-burr, the colly bean: they're both hollow and seamless and have something inside, and they're not made by human hand."

"Neither are they metal," Caidrun countered. "Argue all you like, heynim come from someone's forge."

119

"Then whose?"

"Who can say? But one day I shall trace them backward to their source."

"Hah! Surely that's been tried already?"

"I suppose, unless they came from a place where folk don't go."

Tamborel rolled to face her. "Like the Jagged Mountains?" Where the mist wraiths danced at the edge of the world.

"Why not? There's no one out there to watch the heynim come."

"There's no one out there to make them, either, Caidy."

Caidrun let go a sigh. "I suppose not. But it's a thought, isn't it?"

"An ingenious one," Tamborel murmured. "From the finest mind in Fahwyll."

"You think so?" Caidrun leaned toward him. "Oh, Brel, you will take me to the Gathering?"

Tamborel weighed his answer carefully. "If I thought you really wanted it," he said at last. "But I suspect you only mean to stir things up."

"So you'll be taking Tancey Bider after all?" Caidrun wasn't laughing now. In fact, she looked quite tight and pinched.

"No, Caidy. I shan't even go."

"Not go?" Caidrun clapped her hands. "Oh, won't they just hate it! And won't they hate me, worse than ever!"

"Please, Caidy, don't," Tamborel protested, but she was off again. "And Tancey Bider will be so mad! But let her say one word to me—*one word*!"

"What will you do?"

Caidrun shot him one of her sly smiles. "Wait and see."

Suddenly, Tamborel had had enough. Of pain he couldn't ease; of taunts, imagined slights, and endless, small vendettas. He stood, reaching for his shoes.

"Wait!" Caidrun scrambled up after him, catching at his sleeve. "I've something to show you." She dug into a skirt pocket, pulled out a wad of dark stuff. She shook it out, then let it dangle. It looked like a dead thing, the pulpy carcass of some strange, small animal with shreds of skin or entrails hanging.

Tamborel recoiled. Was this some twisted joke? "What is that?"

She thrust it at him. "Take a look."

The moment his fingers touched it, he cried aloud. It was old, and stained, and half-rotted away, but still recognizable: a helmet, *the* helmet, the very first one. It looked so *small*, thought Tamborel. Yet it had seemed monstrous once. He tugged at one of the fastenings and it came away in his grasp. How many times had he tied and untied those things? He let the fragment fall. "Where did you find it?"

"In an old box. Can you believe Mamma would save such a horror?"

"Why did you bring it, Caidy?" To remind him of

the town's collective guilt? She remembered, surely, how he'd hated the helmets, too. How he'd nagged for years until the grownups said she needn't wear one any more.

Caidrun dipped into her pocket and held out a tinderbox. "I want us to burn it. Make a ceremony, you know?"

Tamborel stared, aghast. "Caidy! We can't strike sparks out here so close to harvest." Fire in this hot, dry time was a constant fear. Only two seasons before, they'd lost five fields of ripe grain to a dry lightning fire.

Caidrun weighed the tinderbox on her palm. "There'll be no danger. Everything's still dripping with rain. Besides, what harm can we do, so close to the brook? Come on, Brel, let's make a pyre."

He held back. "It's just surface wet. And someone will see the smoke."

"How? They're all indoors. Here," she went on, an edge to her voice now, "give me back the helmet. If you won't share, I'll do it by myself."

Tamborel sighed. "All right. But first we clear a patch, right at the water's edge. And we wet a circle all around it."

They scraped clean a wide patch of dirt, laid in its center a small pile of twigs. Then they sprinkled the surrounding earth with water from the brook. Caidrun laid the helmet on the pyre and picked up the tinderbox.

"No, let me." Tamborel took it from her, thinking that if there was to be any trouble, it should fall on him, for Caidy had enough to bear already.

As he bent to make a spark, Caidrun touched his arm. "Wait." She looked up at him earnestly. "We must say something."

"Like what?"

"I don't know." Caidrun looked away. "I'm so tired. Of being here, of being me. Maybe this will change things, if we say the right words."

"Caidy." Tamborel straightened up and hugged her tight, thinking how Hwyllum had treated her just hours before. *My hearth and heart shall evermore be open to her need. . . .* Had his pappa's vow meant nothing? Tamborel released her, kneeling down again. "I know what to say. Listen: Let the bad times go up in flame. Let stiff old casing burn. And let the real Caidy out to spread her wings."

"Oh, Brel." Caidrun looked down, her blue eyes dark, her glistening hair outlined against the sun. "That's lovely. Will it work?"

"Don't see why not."

"I do want to change, I do want people to like me. Is it possible?"

"Anything's possible, Caidy. Now I'm going to strike the spark."

There wasn't much to it. A quick flare, a crackle of twigs, one fleeting puff that gave off a foul and fusty smell, and all that remained was a pile of pale gray ashes. These they kicked with a flourish into the quick currents. For a moment, the specks spun on the surface like fluffy feathers, then they were swept away and swallowed up. While Caidrun stood, staring out, Tamborel smoothed out the burnt patch, doused it, and masked it with stones.

Caidrun turned. "Oh, Brel, I'm such a brat. I cause you so much grief, yet you always understand. I wish there was something I could . . ." With a jingle, one of Caidrun's heynim detached from her cluster and moved to hover over him. Another followed. Then another, and another, then the last: Silwender's gift. "Look up, Brel, pretend they're yours."

He gazed up at the tiny, whirling spheres. Strange, to see them right over his head. He tried to imagine that they really were his, that a nod from his mind could move them where he wished. But he couldn't, and Caidrun's generous gesture only saddened him. "Take them back."

"No. Make music, Brel, go on."

"That I will not! They're not mine to tune!"

"Then I'll set them between us." She took his hand and pulled him down. "Please, sit. Let's share them for a bit. I don't deserve them, anyway. I'm tone-deaf."

"What?" Tamborel slapped his knee. "You're nothing of the sort! You'll make harmony right fine, one day."

"Just as you'll snag heynim, *one day*," Caidrun said.

124

"Aren't we a pair? Look, just for now, I hold, you tune—an even trade. Agreed?"

This was a chance too good to miss. "All right, Caidy."

The golden cluster shifted to hover between them.

"Now, Brel. Make music, now." Caidrun lay back and closed her eyes. Tamborel crossed his legs, then closed his eyes also, shutting out the stony bank and green-black water and radiant evening sky. Then, tuning out all other sounds around him—the stream's rush, a glitter-bug's whine, a flock of purple grain birds' piping—he focused on the heynim's notes. He latched onto Silwender's heyn, slowed its vibrations down. Then he reached for a second, bent its speed to wind around the first. The third he tuned faster, to flash and sparkle in and out of the dominant and secondary harmonies. The fourth, he slowed to a thin, high whine, like the glitter-bug's noontide lay. The fifth, he spun into polyphonic strings of chimes; shimmering notes like glass beads on a wire, spiraling the whole.

Caidrun released a long, contented sigh. He let himself go now, holding the faleyn effortlessly, allowing it to wash through him. Forgiven was their bickering. Forgotten the quarrel with his pappa and the badness that would still be there when he got home.

All the pain, the spite, the wretchedness was gone to ashes, and anything was possible from now on.

·15·

For two days, Tamborel and Hwyllum barely rubbed along. Walking to the fields in silence, they toiled side by side working their sickles up and down the rows of sun-ripe grain stalks, speaking only as was needed. At night, they ate in silence, Eleyna filling in the hole with chatter. Tamborel felt bad, yet he held on for Caidy's sake. Things won't change overnight, he told himself. It would take a while for his words to have effect.

The second evening, after supper, there came a tap at the saba lattice. Tamborel glanced nervously to the kitchen arch. Caidy, come for another confrontation? He ran to head her off.

It was Tancey Bider. Tamborel came on guard. Over a shapely arm was draped a swatch of flowered stuff

126

that fluttered in the evening breeze. "Good evening, Tamborel." Tancey's nod set her heynim dancing. It was a modest cluster, numbering the fingers on one hand, but decent enough for one two years his junior. Her fair, sleek hair gleamed like the ripened grain, her day smock was crisp and fresh even at this late hour.

Eleyna popped up behind him. "Why, Tancey, my dear. What a surprise. Tamborel, show her in. Where are your manners?"

Tancey moved past him into the middle room, shook out the flowery stuff and held it up. "Mistress Eleyna, what do you think?"

"Oh, my dear, what a pretty gown." Eleyna glanced to Tamborel still by the saba. "What do you think, Tam'shu?" Tamborel shrugged, staying put.

"It's for the Harvest Gathering." Tancey spun around, setting the skirts a-swirl. She fetched up before him, awaiting, what? Tamborel held his peace. Tancey smiled up at him, her cheeks round and red and shiny as apples. "We chose the colors especially to match your best suit, Tamborel."

He frowned. "We?"

"My mamma, your mamma—and I." Tancey's smile wavered.

"Why?" Tamborel demanded. "Why would you do that?"

"Perhaps," Eleyna cut in, "we'll speak of that tomorrow."

"Oh, no. Let's speak now." Tamborel didn't *want* a row, didn't want to hurt Tancey Bider, but he would not let them foist this girl upon him. "Tancey, I'm not going to the Harvest Gathering."

"Not—?" Tancey stared, her smile quite gone. "But they said—"

"I'm sorry, but you must find another partner."

Hwyllum strode from the kitchen. "That's no way to talk to Tancey."

"Truth never shamed anyone, Pappa. That's all I'm telling."

Tancey let loose a short, sharp cry. "Now, my dear," Eleyna began, but the damage was done. Their visitor fled, clutching her bundled dress.

Hwyllum and Eleyna turned on him. "How could you!" Eleyna cried.

"Nay," Tamborel retorted. "How could *you*."

"We say you'll go to the feast and with that lass," Hwyllum said angrily. "And while you bide beneath our roof, you'll mind our wishes."

"Oh, don't, Hwyllum." Eleyna turned to Tamborel. "Tam'shu—"

"I'm not your *Tam'shu*!" he burst out. "I'm not a child now—though who would guess it, the way you still treat me?"

Eleyna took his arm. "My dear, we only want what's best for you."

"No, you don't," Tamborel replied bitterly, pulling back. "You want what's best for *you*." Which was whatever was convenient, and respectable. "You, you never really cared for anyone."

"He means Caidrun," Eleyna said quietly.

128

"Oh does he?" Hwyllum sounded grim. "Well, hear this: Your churlishness just now was shameful. You used to be a good son, a fine little boy, tender and obedient. Now look at you—all on account of that, that—"

"Hwyllum!"

"Nay, he's gone too far. From now on, he'll stay clear of Caidrun—and he'll take Tancey Bider to the feast!"

The moment his parents were asleep, Tamborel crept from the house, down the street to Caidrun's. He went around the back, called through her saraba.

She was up in an instant, pulling aside her shutter. "What is it?"

"Pappa has forbidden us to meet. And I'm to take Tancey to the feast."

"But you won't, though?"

"If I don't, it will go all the worse for us."

"Worse than what?"

"It's for a little while, Caidy, until people's tempers die down."

"And when will that be?"

Tamborel stared miserably up at her. "What can I do?"

Caidrun's eyes gleamed. "You could tell them to go jump in the brook."

"How, whilst I bide beneath their roof?"

"By *leaving* it." She leaned out. "Remember what you said? 'Let the real Caidy out to spread her wings.'

Tamborel, I can't do it without you. Please—stand by me. Take me to the feast."

"Pappa will throw me out. What then? I'll be nowhere."

"You're nowhere now." Caidrun backed away into the darkness of her chamber. "Quite the man he looks these days," she called softly. "But he's still Mamma's little boy, keeping to the saba."

Tamborel groaned. "Caidy, we'll show them how you really are, but you must be patient. To defy them now is plain foolishness."

Caidrun's face loomed once more, pale under the starlight. "Wishy-washy hypocrite." She spat the words out. "Spineless, Heynless Wonder. I don't need you, I don't need anyone. I'll show them, I'll show all of you who Caidy really is, just wait and see."

Tamborel awoke with a throbbing head. He would have stayed home that day had it not been for the harvest. He dunked his head in cold water, and set off with Hwyllum, joining the steady stream of men headed for the fields. Tamborel passed Tancey's front yard safely: no Tancey, much to his relief.

The relief was short-lived. Tancey was at the well with a bucket on her arm, in line to draw water. Tamborel dodged out of sight, a move Hwyllum didn't miss. "Be civil," his pappa warned.

As they neared the well, there came a stir: Caidrun, pushing through the waiting women to Tancey's side. The men slowed and a crowd began to form.

130

Tamborel braced himself.

"Good day, Tancey." Caidrun raised a foot and lightly kicked Tancey's pail. "Come to drown your sorrow?"

Tancey flushed. "Come to wash your face?"

"Poor thing." Caidrun smiled sweetly. "Just because Tamborel won't take you to the feast, no need to vent your spleen on me."

Tancey drew herself up. "Tamborel *is* taking me. It's all arranged."

"Between mammas. They told him *after*," Caidrun informed the crowd.

"Well, he isn't taking you, scrawny, grubby thing."

"At least he asked me," Caidrun sneered. "Sleek little pullet, preening your feathers—that no one cares to pluck."

Tancey dropped her bucket with a crash. It rolled, then bounced with a dull clank down the well steps. In the quiet, Tancey drew back her hand and slapped Caidrun's cheek, hard. "Crazy witch. Everyone wishes you'd died."

Tamborel stood, stunned. That Tancey! He ought to dash out and denounce her! But he stayed frozen as in a dream, watching it unfold. Caidrun fingered the weals already forming on her skin. Her eyes on Tancey, she backed toward the well steps.

Caidrun—retreat from trouble? *I'll show them, I'll show all of you who Caidy really is . . .* Tamborel started forward now.

Hwyllum grabbed Tamborel's sleeve and held on.

Caidrun caught the move, shot Tamborel one scathing glance, then, turning back to Tancey, fixed her gaze on a point above Tancey's head. As Tamborel watched in horror, Tancey's heynim left their place and moved across to Caidrun.

"Hey," Hwyllum growled.

The heynim shrank into a solid clump, colliding musically. Then, as everybody watched, the clump rose skyward like a bunch of golden berries.

"What—" Tancey's mouth hung open.

The clump exploded, the heynim shot up all ways, off into the blue.

A hubbub broke out.

Screeching, Tancey lunged at Caidrun but Caidrun danced down the well steps and raced away, laughing. "Make her bring them back!" Tancey shrieked. Mistress Bider ran up, crushed Tancey to her bosom. "Four years it took my Tancey to gather that cluster," she told the crowd. "Now look!"

People were shouting all at once. Rufina pushed her way through, looking distraught. "What is it? What's happened?"

"Your wicked girl has scattered Tancey's cluster!" Mistress Bider cried.

Bennoc climbed the well steps, addressing the crowd. "She does not fear the law, she has no respect for anyone!" The veins in his neck stood out. "Mark my words, this is but the start!"

Tamborel could stand it no longer. "She was provoked! Tancey struck her and called her names."

"Nay," a man called. "Yon hussy started it, taunting Tancey over the feast. She asked for a slapping, plain as day!"

Rufina clutched her chest. "What can I do? Bombrul's in the field."

Yornwey raised her arms for order. "I call a plenary assembly this night. Rufina and Bombrul will bring Caidrun to discuss the matter."

"And then do what we should have done long since," Bennoc cried.

"Aye," the shouts came. "Afore she scatters all our heynim."

Tamborel walked on with Hwyllum, in a roil. Why hadn't Hwyllum stepped in? He could have stopped it, and should, as Caidy's father-mentor. Tamborel shifted his tools to the opposite shoulder. Hwyllum hadn't wanted to stop it. He'd let the quarrel take its course, let her go too far on purpose.

Oh, Caidy! What would they do to her now?

Tamborel thought uneasily of Bennoc's words, Bennoc, who once before had sought to render her blind and deaf. . . . He downed tools and ran to the brook. But Caidrun wasn't there. Had she gone home? he wondered, joining his father back in the field. He very much doubted it: Caidrun was at war.

After work, Tamborel sought her again, but his search proved futile. Supperless, he joined Hwyllum and Eleyna in the Farmer's Hall. So like that other night it was: the heat, the smell, the flickering lamps, the moths. And the air, charged and tight. *Oh, Caidy . . .*

To scatter another's heynim! Never before in all her life had she done ill on purpose. But this was the very worst he could imagine: the ultimate and unpardonable wrong.

Tamborel took his seat before the dais, resolving to speak on her behalf, regardless of Hwyllum, of Bennoc, of them all. He'd tell how she'd resolved to change, to be the way she used to be. "Before they crippled her." He glared around at all the righteous faces, come for trial and judgment. "Whatever they say, she's my friend. The best I have, or want."

He glanced back to the saba uneasily. Folk were growing restless. Shouldn't she have come by now?

Yornwey mounted the dais, but as she raised her arms for silence, Rufina burst in, breathless and beside herself. "We've looked everywhere for Caidrun. We've been along the brook, both banks. But— but—" Rufina bent over, covering her face.

"What my missus is trying to say," Bombrul called out behind her, "is that we can't find Caidrun anywhere."

·16·

In the commotion, Tamborel edged back, through the crowd, and out. Caidrun was hiding. And she'd better stay hid, for now.

"Tamborel?" Meynoc ran out after him. "She made me swear I wouldn't say, but you're the only one she can turn to, me with the missus due any day." Meynoc glanced back to the noisy hall. "She came to us at supper. Demanded food. We gave her all we could spare. Then she took off."

"Took off?" Tamborel echoed stupidly. "Where?"

Meynoc looked grim. "For the Pridicum road."

"The *what*? Why didn't you stop her?"

"And let them drag her here?" Meynoc turned to step back inside. "Go after her, will you? I can't."

Tamborel let out an explosive breath. Two hours

since supper. How far could Caidy have gone in that time? He sprinted to the Y-fork, then right toward the Pridicum road. Reaching his house, Tamborel was forced to slow. He leaned against the open gate, his chest heaving. He'd had no supper. And he was so thirsty, his throat was raw. Dare he stop and pick up a bite? No; they might come looking for him. He set off again, crossed the village boundary, and carried on. Paving gave way to rough track, all ruts and potholes. Tamborel remembered how Hwyllum had run that route years before, fetching Silwender to save Rufina's life. And Caidrun's. *Everyone wishes you'd died...* He staggered, almost went full-length. She must be lost by now. He glanced up at the merest sliver of a moon. He could see no way to follow in this wide dark. Though come to think—there! Still looking up, out of the corner of his eye he detected a faint line curving to the horizon. He looked down, and the line disappeared. So that was it: you kept your eyes *above* the road to see it! Pleased with his discovery, Tamborel   pressed on.

He ran until his legs gave out. Then he walked until his feet burned and he was too weak to take another step. Hardly aware of what he was doing, he tottered off the road, fell under some bushes and closed his eyes.

Sleep came fast. For long, he lay unmoving on the hard, bumpy ground. Then, in the hour before dawn, he dreamed of Caidrun. They sat together by the minnow brook, dabbling their toes in the water. The sky was blue, the sun bright and warm. They got up and strolled along the bank, while the sky deepened and the first stars came out. Caidrun pointed to her cluster. "Tune them to the evening stars, Brel."

Glad of the chance, Tamborel promptly set to, spinning quick, clear, tones as of tinkling crystal. Then, as night fell and the myriad tiny stars emerged, he broke the separate notes and set the chimes a-shimmer.

Caidrun sighed happily. "Beautiful. Oh, Brel, I wish—" She tipped her face to the stars. "I wish," she said softly, "I wish you had all the heynim in the world. Think what you might do with them! Why, you could—"

From way above came a faint, familiar sound as at the monsoons' end when the first heyn-clouds floated over the village. The sounds multiplied, growing nearer, louder. Caidrun gripped his arm. "Brel."

Out of the night they came: first a trickle, then a stream, then a gleaming, golden, chiming river. And the harmonies! Tamborel stood, spellbound, as the endless swarm flowed by, stirring a wind, lifting their hair in its passing.

Beside him, Caidy stirred and laughed out loud.

"I wished for them, and here they are—all the spheres in all the world! Tune them Brel! Tune them now and make us whole!"

Tamborel began to waken slowly, renewed and in a peaceful state.

The peace was short-lived. He'd scarcely stretched and opened his eyes when he heard the sound of angry voices—coming fast. A search party from Fahwyll? Tamborel sat up and peeked out. The homeward track was empty. Ahead, it led to a rise. As he looked, figures crested the rise: some half-dozen men, jogging at a lick. Tamborel ducked down.

As the men approached, their voices came quite clear.

"How do we know she didn't hail from Minavar, Nostur?"

"Because those children saw her come over this rise."

The men were almost level now. Tamborel could hear their labored breathing. He peeked again, and froze: four of them were heynless!

"All this talk of where she *come* from, Nostur," one man puffed. "She took off in the opposite direction. We're headed the wrong way!"

"No, we're not." Nostur mopped his brow. "Our heynim are gone, she's gone. But she's from Fahwyll, and someone's child . . . those folk . . . make good our loss. . . ." Their voices faded.

Tamborel crept out. Caidy! Had she gone quite mad? Venting her wrath on Tancey Bider was one thing. But on Pridicum folk? He made for the rise.

Pridicum turned out to be a small town, with large, two-storied houses and a wide main street, noisy with children. As Tamborel neared, they stopped

138

their games and fled. In no time, grownups ran out to surround him.

"They say you came from that way." A man pointed back toward the rise.

The man looked hostile, menacing. Tamborel swallowed. "I did."

"There! You see? He's with the girl!" A knuckly hand closed on Tamborel's arm.

"Girl?" Tamborel thought fast. "Was she small, skinny, and all bushy hair?" He pointed up. "I've chased her all the way from Fahwyll. Scattered my heynim, she did. Look." All eyes went to the vacant space above his head. "And I'm not the only one!" he went on, sounding angry. "I've to catch her before she does more harm. Which way did she go?"

The hand shook him roughly. "Nay, we ask the questions. Come along." They began to drag him down the street.

"Wait." Tamborel pulled back. What if they locked him up? He'd never find Caidy at this rate. Oh, what to do? Casinder! Tamborel scanned the faces. The zjarn would vouch for him. But he'd never recognize the man after all this time—unless . . . He closed his eyes and listened. Yes, near the back of the crowd: Tamborel would know that cluster anywhere. "Casinder, sir! Remember me? I'm Hwyllum's son. You woke me from my sleep!"

Casinder came forward and eyed him up and down. "Yes, I remember." He turned to the crowd.

"Gentle folk, this young man is no rogue, but the good son of a respectable man. I'm taking him home with me." The zjarn led Tamborel down the street to his big, airy house where he lived alone. He gave Tamborel breakfast, enough for three. Then sat, elbows on the table, watching. In the silence, the man's heynim circled lazily about his head, their jingle muted. Tamborel did not heed them much at first, for he was too intent upon the hollow in his middle. But as that hole began to fill, Tamborel eased up, letting the peaceful sounds wash through, loosening his knots. Presently, he leaned back, letting out a sigh.

Casinder spoke. "This girl: she has much power. Is she who I think?"

"Maybe," Tamborel answered cautiously. "What exactly did she do here?"

"They claim she scattered four clusters, unprovoked. But the truth is that this morning at first light she begged food from four houses and was chased away. She's Bombrul's daughter, isn't she?"

"Yes."

"I knew it!" The zjarn slapped his palm down on the table. Then he looked up, clearly puzzled. "You said she took your heynim also."

"I . . . lied. Though she did steal someone else's— but only after she was driven to it," he added with some spirit.

Casinder shook his head slowly. "I can't believe

that anyone would do such a thing, however badly goaded. Whatever has made her like this?"

Tamborel told how they had shut Caidrun away and made her wear the helmet. "So she grew up deaf to the chimes—at the very age she should have had them all around her. At least, that's what I think."

"And you are right," Casinder said grimly. "You mean to tell me that Yornwey, your zjarn, agreed to this barbaric treatment? Barbaric—and stupid. Why did they not take her to see Silwender?"

Tamborel explained, about the High Zjarn's fees, Fahwyll's depleted coffers. As he spoke, Casinder sighed and shook his head repeatedly, setting his heynim cloud a-shake. "Money isn't everything. Silwender would have helped Caidrun, if they'd asked. He's a kind and gentle man. Look at the heyn he sent at her naming." Casinder shot Tamborel a look. "But tell me, what of your heynim? Where are they?"

Tamborel looked down at his empty plate. "I never had any."

Casinder leaned forward. "I do not understand."

"I cannot snag."

Casinder looked sharp. "What does Yornwey say to this?"

Tamborel frowned. "Why, nothing."

"She never tried to find the reason out?"

"Could she have?"

The zjarn looked totally disgusted now. "One would have thought so. If you like, I maybe could—"

"Thank you," Tamborel said. "But first I must find Caidy."

Casinder's brows went up. "I see. Well, maybe that's wise. There's no telling how she might go. Where will you look?"

"Where does the road lead?"

"It runs westward for a full morning's stride, then it splits three ways. Take the middle road to Minavar. That's a good two days' journey. When you get there, go to the Hon'faleyn and ask for Silwender."

"But it's Caidy I'm after."

"Exactly. That's where I'd go to find her. If she's not there, the High Zjarn will tell you what to do." Casinder reached across the table for his hand. "While you're there, tell Silwender of your own affliction. Being heynless is not natural. I myself have never heard of such a thing. He'll likely find the reason and maybe even the cure. So don't be foolish like the rest of Fahwyll: ask his help." He let go Tamborel's hand and stood. "You're itchy to be off, that's plain. I'll pack you some food and see you to the edge of town."

·17·

It took two days to get to Minavar. As Tamborel climbed the hill on which the Hall of Harmonies stood, the early-morning sun reflected off the high stone walls and cast blue shadow under the entrance gate.

Beside the gate was a watchman's box. In it sat a man: small, hunched, with graying forelock. As Tamborel made for the gate, the man scuttled out to bar his way, his heynim bobbing. "And just where are you going?" Tamborel noted with interest a couple of larger-sized heynim in the man's cluster.

"You haven't let a girl through here? Not so tall." Tamborel raised his hand shoulder-high. "Skinny. Blue eyes, dark, bushy hair."

"You know how many folk pass through here each day?" The man cocked his head. "You're foreign, aren't you? Of course you are or you'd not ask such a daft question. Know what this place is?"

"Yes." Tamborel tried another tack. "I wish to see the High Zjarn."

"You do? Then I'll see your pass." The man held out his hand.

Tamborel stared at the empty palm. Pass? "I haven't one. But I must see Silwender. It's urgent."

The gatekeeper nodded. "That's what they all say. Sorry. No one goes past me without the wherewithal."

"But I—I've come a long way—"

"So has everybody. If you're sick, I need a token from your zjarn. If you want to be a novice—" The man shrugged. "Go home, lad. Only the best get in to learn the harmonies. I've turned back folk with swarms too great to count, while you—" The man broke off. "You haven't . . . one . . . single . . ."

Tamborel leapt in. "That's why I'm here! Silwender will see me. He knows me. In fact, if he finds you keep me out here, there'll be trouble."

"Trouble?" The gatekeeper looked doubtful. "I'll call the Steward." He stepped into his box and pulled a rope. Somewhere above, a bell clanged, bringing a portly man, in velvet and brocade.

"Now what, Kowl?" His cluster chimed crisply.

"This here lad claims to know the High Zjarn, sir. Wants to see him. But he has no pass."

144

The Steward looked Tamborel up and down. "No pass?"

"Nor no heynim, neither."

"No heynim? But that's—" The man eyed Tamborel with interest now.

"And in view of recent, er, *troubles*"—he lingered on the word—"I thought it wise to call you."

"Yes, yes." The Steward glanced back to the courtyard behind him. "If this is some trick, boy, you'll be sorry," he warned. "Follow me."

Tamborel paced the waiting room. People came in from time to time to ask his name and errand. Each time he said, "I'm Hwyllum's son from Fahwyll. I'm here to see Silwender." He finished off Casinder's rations. Once, he even dozed. Finally, the Steward reappeared. "Come."

The man walked Tamborel through halls and galleries filled with chiming from passersby trailing huge swarms. "Hurry," he urged, as Tamborel slowed in fascination. "Move along, Silwender waits."

Silwender waits! Tamborel felt a rush of excitement. To meet the High Zjarn face to face—after all these years! He dimly remembered silver hair and a flowing beard. He still saw the eyes clearly, though. Who could forget that piercing look! Tamborel pictured the old man's swarm as he remembered it from that day, trailing the length of the village street almost to the Y-fork. That night, those wondrous heynim had filled Rufina's chamber, thick as sun-bugs massed for fall migration. Would the swarm seem as vast, would it sound as powerful to him now that he was grown?

Tamborel quickened his pace.

Silwender's private chamber was up a high turret with a narrow, worn stone stair wide enough for only one. As they climbed those steps in single file, Tamborel's skin began to prickle in a strange, familiar way.

Atop the stair was a small wooden door. The Steward knocked and waited.

"Come." The voice was dry and wavery.

The room was tiny: bare stone walls, a narrow, high saraba letting in a flood of light. Silwender sat in an armchair with high, fan-shaped back. Overhead, heynim swarmed like a dazzling aura, coiling above the rafters up into the turret's cone. Tamborel shut his eyes and covered his ears, feeling giddy. Hands steadied his shoulders. The onslaught faded to a distant chiming. Tamborel opened his eyes. The heynim hovered, muted. The Steward was gone. "Here. Sit." The old man pointed to a footstool by his chair. Silwender was smaller and frailer than Tamborel had expected. But he'd remembered the hair aright—and the eyes. "You are Hwyllum's son? You wish to see me, I understand." He glanced to the space above Tamborel's head.

"Yes, sir." Tamborel sat gratefully. "About Caidrun, Rufina's daughter. Do you remember her? You sent her a heyn to mark her naming."

"What about her?"

"Is she in the Hon'faleyn?"

Silwender frowned slightly. "Should she be?"

"Casinder said—I thought—" Tamborel stood up.

Silwender waved him down again. "Take a breath, young man. Sit. Now, one word at a time, tell me what this is about."

Tamborel sighed. "Caidrun's in trouble, though it's not her fault. And I must find her before something *really* dreadful happens."

The High Zjarn folded his arms. "This trouble wouldn't have to do with scattering heynim? Aha, I thought so. You'd better tell me more. When did this trouble truly start? Not in this past day or so, I'll wager."

"No, sir. It's been coming almost since she was born." Tamborel told of Caidrun's first anniversary; how she'd snagged heynim to her, how he'd saved her, of his injuries. Of the plenary meeting and the judgment on Caidrun. The old man sat, motionless, though his heynim shook as Tamborel told of Bennoc's plan to blind and deafen Caidrun. But he did not speak until Tamborel had finished telling of the hated helmet and how folk had shunned her. And how finally Tancey Bider had slapped her face and called her "witch" and said how everybody wished that she had died.

"So. This is a bad business. Very bad all around." Silwender looked at Tamborel from under his brows. "She didn't scatter your heynim, did she?"

"No, sir. I haven't any to scatter."

"Say again?"

Tamborel sighed. He felt such shame to tell it. "I cannot snag. I want to, but there's something stopping me—though I can tune real fine. Casinder said that you might be able to—" He stopped, recalling why he was there. "He said that Caidrun would come here, to the Hall of Harmonies. And if not, that you'd tell me what to do."

Silwender shifted in his chair, stroking his fine, silver beard. "She arrived in Minavar yesterday, but she did not come here. There were several incidents, I was informed, but I had no idea who she was."

A day ahead of him! "Is she in Minavar still, sir?"

"Who knows? Folk are searching, but so far no one's caught her."

Tamborel got to his feet. "I must go."

"Go where, boy?" Silwender shook his head. "Those are angry folk out there. Folk who know the city. If they can't find her, you certainly will not. Let me think . . ." Silwender sat back in his chair and closed his eyes. Several large-sized heynim floated down to frame his head, their deep notes sounding out above the rest. Despite his anxiety, Tamborel felt his body give. He leaned forward on his stool, propping his chin in his hands, watching, listening. His eyes began to close. . . .

"I agree with Casinder." Silwender's voice.

Tamborel opened his eyes and stretched, feeling

wondrously refreshed, as if he'd slept—for how long? "Sir?"

"Caidrun's gift will draw her to the Hon'faleyn eventually, though when I cannot say. So you must go back home and I'll send word when she turns up."

Go home? "With all respect, sir, I must stay and find her."

"And how will you live, young man?"

"I'll manage, somehow. It will not be for long."

Silwender sighed. "You do not know the city. Look, you'll sleep here tonight, then tomorrow—well, we'll see."

·18·

They found him a berth in the novice quarters. The cell was narrow, and bare save for twin double bunks along each side wall. Facing the door was a small saraba bright with mid-afternoon sun. Left alone, Tamborel crossed the room and looked out westward. A sea of rooftops vanished into haze. Beyond, on the skyline, pale gray spikes marked a misty range. He leaned out. Were they, they had to be the Jagged Mountains where the mist wraiths danced: the edge of the world! They certainly looked mysterious and forbidding, just as in those merchants' tales. Propping his elbows on the sill, he recalled how, long ago, he'd told them to Caidy. How only nights before they'd argued over whether heynim could have come from those mountains or no. Tamborel let out a sigh. If only Caidy were there to share this sight.

He leaned out farther now, peering down onto nearby roofs beneath which dark streets twisted like tangled yarn. Was Caidy still in Minavar? They said not, but then they did not know her. She might well be down there still, dodging, staying hid in spite of all their searches. Tamborel clenched his fists, recalling the scene at the well: Caidy's angry face, the bright red weals across her cheek. The look she'd thrown him. "I'll not go home until I find you, however long it takes," he growled.

Quick steps sounded outside. The door opened, three youths burst through and pulled up in surprise. "Hello." The foremost of the group, tall, with long face, long, thin nose, strong black brows and wavy hair curling down onto broad shoulders, came forward a step more. His eyes went to the space above Tamborel's head and stayed. "Are you lost?" He seemed friendly enough.

"I was put here. For the night." All three, Tamborel couldn't help but see, held clusters as large as Yornwey's, with some bigger heynim, too.

The dark-haired youth nodded. "Well, I'm Jareyd." He turned to the others. "He's Keiryn. And he's Hewl." Keiryn was even taller than Jareyd, but thin and stooped, with pale, pitted skin and lank brown hair falling over one eye. At mention of his name, he tossed back his wayward locks, revealing a brow so high and narrow it looked *squeezed*. "Glad to meet you," he said, then smiled, and Tamborel took to him at once. Hewl, a stocky towhead with raw, red face that made him look angry, reached but to Jareyd's shoulder. "So what's your name?" Hewl said, his pale eyes bright with challenge.

"Tamborel, of Fahwyll."

"Fahwyll?" The boys looked at one another.

"It's east of Pridicum," Tamborel explained.

The boys looked no less at a loss.

"What are you doing here?" Hewl's question was a challenge.

"You needn't answer," Jareyd said, throwing Hewl a warning glance.

"It's all right. I'm looking for a girl."

Hewl looked arch. "A girl? What made you think she'd come here?"

"Casinder—a zjarn—said that she might."

Keiryn spoke up. "She's gifted, then?"

"Yes. No."

"Aha! The mystery deepens." Hewl climbed onto the upper right-hand bunk and sat, swinging his well-muscled legs. "How did you get past old Coal Bucket at the gate? And who let you stay the night?"

"Hewl!" Jareyd turned to Tamborel. "Here, take my bunk." The upper left-hand bunk, across from Hewl. Without waiting for Tamborel's reply, Jareyd threw himself onto the cot beneath. Suddenly, Keiryn spoke. "She's the one they seek: the heynim-scatterer."

Jareyd laughed at Tamborel's startled face. "Isn't he a riot? Keiryn reads minds, which can be a nuisance, I tell you. He's going to be a zjarn."

A zjarn! Tamborel eyed Keiryn in awe.

"Never mind about all that," Hewl said. "What happened to your heynim? Did this weird girl scatter them, too?"

Tamborel hesitated. "N-no. I never had any." Best to get it over with, much as he hated to admit it.

"You don't say! But that's—"

"Hewl, let him be!" Jareyd sat up. "Excuse him, he's new and brash and doesn't know his manners. Like how to treat those . . ." He faltered.

"Those less fortunate, he wants to say, but hasn't the nerve." Hewl grinned. "To hold *no* heynim is quite some feat. How do you do it?"

Heat flashed to Tamborel's face—then fizzled. There was no malice in Hewl's eyes, he saw that now. The boy was simply quizzing him. And that made him feel more at home than all this polite talk. Why, Hewl's bluntness felt easy as old shoes: was he not inured to it from a boyhood spent with Meynoc and the other boys? "If only I knew," he said, shrugging.

Hewl pressed on. "I mean, you look normal enough. Yet even the simplest folk hold one or two." He swung his legs up onto his bunk and lay back. "I cannot imagine how it would be, to have no feel for chimes at all."

"Oh, but I have that," Tamborel cried, stung. "I can tune a faleyn."

"A *faleyn*?" Hewl was up again. "How, without a schooling in the Basal Harmonics? Even we novices don't learn to tune the simplest faleyn until our second year. And, anyway, how could you do it without a cluster?"

"The girl I'm seeking—she let me use hers."

"And you tuned it, I suppose?" The boy looked frankly skeptical.

Why, Hewl thought him a liar! Now Tamborel was rattled at last.

"Words get us nowhere," Keiryn said. "Let Tamborel prove his claim. Here." The boy sent his cluster across the narrow space to bob by Tamborel's head. So. Tamborel looked at all the boys in turn. Keiryn was of a mind with Hewl. And likely so was Jareyd, for all the show of courtesy. These privileged students of the Hon'faleyn would put him, the rank outsider, to the test as did the boys in Fahwyll when he begged their acceptance?

Well, so be it!

Tamborel climbed up onto his borrowed bunk and surveyed the unfamiliar cluster. The tones were well matched, he found. In among the small heynim were three middle-sized and two big ones. He pointed to the last. "We never see those in Fahwyll.

Are they more powerful than the smaller ones, Keiryn?"

Keiryn flipped back his hair. "No. All are part of the whole, as is the nature of harmony. Do you know their names? The smallest are intyl; the middle ones, anintyl; the largest are omantyl."

Tamborel repeated the names slowly. *"Intyl. Anintyl. Omantyl."* No one in Fahwyll had even heard those names, not even Yornwey.

"So now you know," Hewl said loudly. "Will you get on with it?"

Tamborel nodded, shifting his legs, making himself comfortable. As he moved, the cluster jingled musically. Oh, if only it were his! Its nearness brought back the evening by the minnow brook, when he and Caidrun had shared such peace. . . . He could not weave those glad harmonies now. In fact, he wondered if he ever would again. *Oh, Caidy!*

He reached out, focused on the two omantyl. He set them rolling on a common axis to form a sort of sound rod for which they formed the poles: Tamborel and Caidrun, bound together, held apart. Then, taking each anintyl in turn, he set them spinning to chime with each pole in sequence, pointing up their separation. Finally, he scattered the tiny intyl, dropping their peals like tears into the winding helix. . . .

As Tamborel spun the sound strands, he forgot himself, forgot the boys, and that he was proving himself. All was sadness, and pain, and deep remorse. Caidy... Oh, he couldn't bear it! Out there, forsaken and abandoned.

Caidy, you are not alone. I'll seek you, even to the world's end. . . .

Hewl was the first to stir. He cleared his throat and blew his nose. "What a weird faleyn. Where did you find it? Not in any Table, I'll bet."

"Tamborel has no need of the old Tables. He'll be writing new ones." Keiryn summoned back his cluster, Tamborel heard it go and felt a pang.

"What did you see, Hewl?" Keiryn asked, but Hewl, grunting, only turned away. "I saw my grandfather," Keiryn volunteered dreamily. "We used to be so close. No one else had time for me. He took me for walks, he told me marvelous stories, adventures that went on forever. When he died, I hated him for deserting me." Keiryn lay down and turned to face the wall.

"I remembered summers when I was small," said Jareyd. "Life was good then. The days seemed long as a whole year and we never went to bed. I had a friend called Marcur. He moved away. I thought it was because of me, because I always made us stay out far too late." Sighing, he lay down also, and curled up into himself.

The sun went down, the room filled up with dusk. Tamborel leaned back and closed his eyes, deep into the past few days. And thus they all stayed, bound into a common silence, until the supper bell.

Next morning, Silwender sent for him. "Caidrun is not found. Go home. I'll send word when we have her."

"No! I must wait here!"

"But what of your parents?"

What, indeed? thought Tamborel. If they'd rejected Caidrun, they'd rejected him, too. "If you send me away, I'll not go back to Fahwyll."

"Oh?" The High Zjarn stroked his silky beard with fine, dry, tapered fingers. "Jareyd claims you tuned a faleyn last night. Is this some novice foolery?"

Tamborel looked down. "No, sir."

"I see. Well, we'll look into it, presently. If Jareyd speaks true, then perhaps you'll bide a while and learn something, at least, until Caidrun comes. As for your folk, I'll send word now to tell them that you're safe and in good hands—that is, if you don't object," he added dryly.

"No, sir." Tamborel could scarcely speak the words. He, in the Hall of Harmonies! Maybe if he proved his worth, when Caidy came they'd both stay on and learn along with Jareyd, Keiryn, Hewl, and all the rest!

·19·

Next morning, after breakfast, Tamborel sat in on a novice class, some dozen or so boys and girls around his age, including Hewl, and Jareyd, and Keiryn. Awed by the size of the students' clusters, he sat in a back corner, feeling useless and conspicuous while the students strove to adjust their heynim's pitch by varying the speed of rotation. This they did by counting the degrees aloud, overshooting then pulling back. At first, he thought this was what they were supposed to do, but as he watched, he realized that their overshooting was an error and they were trying unsuccessfully to correct it. Awe gave way to puzzlement. How could they be so *clumsy*? Tamborel inched

158

his chair forward. Why did they count rotations by degrees, anyway? He could simply *sense* the pitch and rate of spin the way he knew how hot or cold or hungry he was. It was all he could do not to leap up and show them!

Rawl, the tutor, seemed quite satisfied, however. "Good. Now: select a single heyn, try to reverse its spin suddenly and see what happens."

The novices moved to obey, but their heynim continued to rotate in the same direction. Only Keiryn and a tall girl with three omantyl in her cluster succeeded, after a fashion. For a few seconds, each small sphere floated, motionless, then began to revolve in the opposite direction.

"That's right," Rawl said. "Now, Keiryn, Synla: try again, and this time make your reversal *sharp*." As the class watched, the two repeated the exercise once, twice, then several times until, at last, Synla succeeded.

For an instant, as the heyn snapped into reverse spin, Tamborel caught a faint sound way above the chime, a sort of whining hum as at home when cold spring winds keened through the narrow space between houses. He frowned, trying to remember, sure that he'd heard that sound before somewhere.

"Very good, Synla. You've just produced phantom harmonics—ghost chimes," Rawl said. "Overtones that increase a heyn's power one-hundredfold. As you heard, they last no more than the space of a spark, so whatever you want to achieve with them, be quick about it. Continue."

Tamborel edged his chair out even farther. Another minute, and he'd burst. If only *he* had heynim to work with! Oh, how he would like to try!

Rawl paused by Tamborel's chair. A big man, with kindly, weathered face, grizzled hair and beard, looking more like a farmer than a Fellow in the Hon'faleyn—except for the great swarm circling above him. "I hope you're enjoying your visit with us." His eyes went to the space over Tamborel's head. "Though I suppose it's mainly hard to just sit by and watch."

Tamborel nodded. Rawl spoke true—but not in the way he intended.

The door opened.

Silwender entered.

The novices stopped their practice, pulling in their clusters. The High Zjarn shot Jareyd a keen look from under his fine, arched brows, then addressed the class. "If I have been informed correctly, our visitor from Fahwyll has something to share with us. Tamborel, you will please step out."

Tamborel froze, clean forgetting how only moments before he'd barely refrained from leaping up to demonstrate. Now, with all eyes upon him, he decided that he'd rather reveal his skill in more secluded fashion, say, atop Silwender's high stone stair.

Silwender beckoned him forward. "How big a cluster would you like?"

How big? Tamborel wouldn't know. "About this many." He held up both hands, fingers spread. Nodding, the old man turned to the novices, quelling scattered sniggers. "You will sit, and be still." As they obeyed, the High Zjarn detached a cluster from his swarm and sent them across to Tamborel. A gasp from the novices now, quickly stifled. Tamborel forgot his fright. Silwender's own heynim! Intyl, mostly; two anintyl and *three* wondrous deep and mellow omantyl. He gazed up, smitten by their beauty. They reminded him of Eleyna's flower beds at the height of summer, especially the anemones: small bright gems, their vibrant colors snagging passersby. . . . A garden, that was it. He'd spin a garden of delight, filled with brilliant chiming!

"You should have seen Silwender's face!" Jareyd exclaimed, the moment they got to their room. "Truly, he was amazed."

"Don't exaggerate," Hewl said. "Let us say he was somewhat impressed. What did he tell you afterward, Tam-boy?"

"That he's to stay on as a novice, of course," Keiryn said. "Is that not so, friend?"

Tamborel walked past them to the saraba and stood, gazing out over city and empty plain to the distant mountains beyond, hugging the memory of that interview to himself a moment longer.

" . . . You will live and study with the rest. Learn the

Tables of Basal Harmonics, and the Books of Lore, and all the fields of application with the other novices. But you'll learn to tune your faleyn here, in my chamber, with such heynim as I provide. Agreed?"

Live and study with the rest? Tune his faleyn with Silwender? He, a farmer's son, enrolled into the Hall of Harmonies by the High Zjarn himself? Many times Tamborel had pictured this unlikely occasion. How glad he'd feel, and proud. But at that moment all he felt was guilt. He had no business to be there. He was supposed to be seeking Caidy. It didn't seem right that the search worked to his great good while she was still at large.

"What about Caidrun?"

The old man's eyes gleamed. "You think her fate is in your hands now? That we could afford to waste such gifts? Once she comes, we'll bring her to a proper state of mind. After that, we'll see." Silwender gave him a little push. "So now go along. We'll begin work together in due course. Meantime, I've sent again to your parents, letting them know that you're a student here now. And I've invited them to visit you at any time they wish."

On his way down that narrow stair, Tamborel had felt quite numb. But now he felt a surge of joy, like the rush of blood to a limb that has been sat on for too long. He turned from the saraba. "I'm to be your roommate, if that's all right with you."

"Wonderful!" Jareyd cried, clapping Tamborel on the shoulder. "Though you'll take the lower bunk now."

"Shall you be a novice, or what?" Hewl demanded. "Considering your *prodigious* talent."

"I shall." Tamborel's spirits surged higher still.

"But how, without a cluster?"

"I'm to tune with Silwender."

Hewl whistled. "One week, and Tam-boy will be too grand for us!"

Tamborel grinned, pointing up. "Caidrun calls me the Heynless Wonder. It's a great leveler, so you won't have to watch out for my cap size."

"Did Silwender say if he can heal you?" Jareyd asked.

"No. We had too much else to talk about."

Hewl clicked his tongue. "Too bad, Tam-boy. So ask him tomorrow."

"He won't," said Keiryn. "Not until Caidrun's found."

"What did Silwender say about her? She's in for trouble, I'll bet."

"No, Hewl," Tamborel said defensively. "She only scattered a few heynim. It's not the worst crime in the world."

"Actually, it is, just about." Jareyd looked almost apologetic. "It says so in the very first Book of Lore. Perla read it to us just last week."

"Perla?"

"Our reading tutor."

"She's a *tyrant*, watch out!"

"Hewl!" Keiryn spoke up. "She's strict, Tamborel. But also fair, and very patient. She reads beautifully, and never makes you feel the dunce."

"Good old Keiryn," Hewl said. "Finding good in everyone. As Jareyd was about to say, the text goes 'While one may vie for unsnagged heynim, one may not appropriate another's cluster, either to steal, or to scatter it. Neither may one broach a single heyn, whatever its condition.' "

" 'Broach'?"

"It means you can't dig them up once they're buried, or take them apart to see inside. And you especially cannot harm the ones in use. Know why? Because," Hewl went on without a pause, 'Heynim hold the world in being.' "

"They do?" Tamborel glanced out of the saraba. Maintain that vast city, that great, wide plain, those mountains and the skies above them? All Alyafaleyn itself! He scanned his roommates closely. Surely they were teasing. And yet . . . chimes helped grow good crops and ensure fair weather, and they healed sickness, too. "You are serious."

"Indeed," Keiryn said quietly. "It's the first statement in the Book of Mysteries. Put simply, it says that heynim are what hold us in existence. As long as they keep chiming, Alyafaleyn goes on. But if one day they should fail, our world and everything in it will perish."

164

"So, as I said, that girl is in for it." Hewl was goading him again.

"Don't listen," said Jareyd. "Silwender will take care of her."

Tamborel hoped so. He thought back to the High Zjarn's words. *You think her fate is in your hands now? That we could afford to waste such gifts?* "You're right," he said. "In fact, she's to be a novice, too."

The next day, Tamborel began studying to read and write and count. He pored over meaningless squiggles on parchment, feeling much ashamed. But Perla, a tall, thin woman with long, curved neck and black hair piled atop her head, sat with him and took out a small slate. For two hours, she drew bold, curly characters, which Tamborel copied, learning their names by heart. By the end of the lesson, he was reading a few simple words. Perla smiled. "Tamborel, you'll catch up with the class in no time." He felt his color come and go. He'd done well? And enjoyed himself into the bargain. Oh, this was the place to be!

Tamborel gazed around the room at shelves stacked with scrolls and fat books bound in leather. So many! To think that most folk outside never even saw a single one. Keiryn came up behind him. "I told you Perla was all right," he said. "She's very pleased with you, I can tell."

While the other novices went on to work with Rawl, Tamborel stayed behind with Perla. Under her calm and patient guidance he learned fast, growing more confident each day. By the end of the week, he was reading whole sentences. *Me*, he thought when he went to sleep at night. A son of the grainfields, learning to read, and write, and tally numbers. Not even Yornwey can read letters or count the heynim in her cluster! And any day now he'd start tuning with the High Zjarn!

But it was two weeks before Silwender summoned Tamborel up his stair. "Ah, come in. The messenger is back from Fahwyll. Hwyllum and Eleyna say to tell you they love you and are proud of you. They regret they cannot visit in the midst of harvest, but they hope to come after the monsoons. You don't look happy, boy. What is it?"

"They'll not come," said Tamborel. "There'll be sowing and ditches to clear. There's always something."

"Well, they can't help that, Tamborel. So don't leap to judgment, eh? We all must live as best we can. Now, to another matter."

"Caidy?" Tamborel pounced. "You've found Caidy?"

Silwender shook his head. "Not yet, my boy. Sit down."

Tamborel took his place on the footstool at Silwender's feet.

"It's not about Caidrun. It's about you and your affliction: I want to help you, if I can."

"*If* you can, sir?"

"It will depend on you."

"How?"

"You must desire it."

Desire it! How could there be any doubt? "I want to be healed, to be made right and whole. I'm sick to have my swarm."

"Really. Well, let's see." Silwender picked up a small rolled mat beside his chair, shook it out, and laid it between them. "Get you down, go on," he urged, as Tamborel hesitated. "You're not afraid?"

"Oh no. Why should I be?" Tamborel stretched full length on the mat and closed his eyes. Come to think, he did feel nervous, who wouldn't? He heard the creak of the High Zjarn's chair, the rustle of his robes. "Relax, my boy, and for pity's sake breathe, or you'll expire before I've tuned a single note!" Tamborel unclenched his fists and breathed in deep. "That's better. Now let yourself go, eh?"

Silwender began to tune, starting in the bottom register, then sliding up. So many varied tones, such subtle differences in timbre! Any other time, Tamborel would have lain entranced by the richness of it all. But for some reason his heart began to race. *What did Silwender mean to do?*

"I sense great fear. Calm down, boy." The old man's voice sounded far away. "Slow your blood, open yourself to the chiming. Don't think: *feel.*"

Tamborel took deep, slow breaths, letting go. . . .

An image filled his mind: of glistening filaments coiling into one thick string, then snaking down through dark with blind and questing head. He had an image of the slow worm in the minnow brook, parasitic larva of the flit fly. It rode the currents seeking out an unsuspecting host. Lighting on the hapless minnow, it slipped through the fish's gills and burrowed deep inside.

His mind snapped to, his body stiffened. He couldn't breathe, pain seized his chest like wire. "Stop! Stop!"

Silwender broke the faleyn instantly and with such force Tamborel's ears sang and everything went dark. When he came to again, he still lay on the mat, Silwender still sat in his chair, watching him. "Ha. So. Stay a minute longer, then come up easy, boy."

"What happened?" Even as Tamborel asked, he knew. *Phantom harmonics—nicknamed ghost chimes . . . overtones that increase a heyn's power one-hundred-fold . . .* Silwender's ghost chimes, that he'd heard long years before, lying underneath Rufina's sill. Now once again they had assailed his senses with full force— and he'd resisted them! *How?* How had he done that—and *why?*

Silwender helped him sit up. "What happened, sir?" Tamborel slumped forward, his head in his hands.

"You would not let my faleyn do its work."

"You mean I fought the healing? Why? Why would I do that?"

168

Silwender spread his fine, dry hands. "People deny themselves for many different reasons. Self-hate, perhaps. Guilt. Or fear."

"Fear?" Fear of being cured?

"Sometimes it's a case of 'better the affliction we know than the cure we don't.' Only this spring a woman begged me to try to heal her blindness of many years' standing. Then she resisted me, as fiercely as you did now."

"Did you cure her, sir?"

"Only after she realized that while she wanted to see, she was also very much afraid of what would meet her eyes."

"Do you think that's me? That I want healing and that I also fear it, at one and the same time?"

"It's highly possible. I did sense fear in you."

"But of what, sir? Not heynim, or I'd not be tuning them, would I?"

Silwender stroked his beard thoughtfully. "Whatever, it's deeply hid. It may take some time for us to find it out."

Deeply hid. Tamborel thought of the questing worm and shivered. "But we will, in the end?"

"When you so wish it, boy."

·20·

Tamborel studied hard, keen to catch up with the other novices, yet not entirely immersed as he might have been. From time to time, in those early weeks, whenever anyone came into class with a whispered message for the teacher, Tamborel would come alert, sure that the message was for him, and that Caidy had come at last.

But as the weeks passed, and still she did not appear, Tamborel grew more and more absorbed in his studies until sometimes he scarcely thought of her until he was abed and drifting off to sleep. He had not dreamed that there could be so much to learn, about the world, and the heynim, and those who tuned them. One day, Rawl led the class to an innermost courtyard surrounded by four high, slender turrets.

"Now you all know something of tuning heynim, hear this: one *tunes* a *cluster*, but one *spins* a *swarm*. Listen."

For a moment, Tamborel heard nothing but the usual clamor of chimes floating out through myriad sarabas, mingling in the high air. Then all at once, the sound of chimes burst upon them from somewhere close, filling the courtyard with rich, melodious echoes. Tamborel wheeled full circle, looking to each high turret. Yes, the chimes came from not one, but all four of them.

Rawl pointed. "Up there sit the Sky Spinners, easing us through into fall, keeping at bay the winds and rains until all the crops are gathered in and folk are safely latched inside their houses."

Tamborel gazed up at the narrow, arched sarabas, wishing he could see those Spinners at their work. "How many Spinners are there, sir?"

Rawl looked pleased at the question. "They number twelve in all, and are divided into three tetrads. The first tetrad spins to the sky, the second to the earth, and the last to our general state of well-being."

"Are there any more Spinners outside the Hon'faleyn?" asked Synla.

Rawl shook his head. "Only these twelve. They split their day into three watches, and take turns to help keep our world in balance. You just heard the

Sky Spinners begin their watch. However, in times of emergency, all the Spinners work around the clock until the general harmony is restored."

Tamborel listened, enthralled. No longer did he wish to be a zjarn. He pictured himself, sitting up in one of those high turrets, spinning his vast swarm, sending healing harmonies across the high air; chimes that carried all the way to Fahwyll without his having to stir!

The days grew short. Layer upon layer of thick gray cloud gradually piled up over the city, bearing ever lower under its own weight, until the Hon'faleyn turrets were wreathed in mist. Lamps were lit. Men sealed the sarabas with stout steel shutters, transforming the sunlit halls into a labyrinth of gloomy caves and passages. To Tamborel, the Hon'faleyn took on the air of a fortress preparing for a siege, a comfortable one with no danger in it. He thought of the folk in Fahwyll shutting up their tiny houses, already under one another's feet. Here, in the Hall of Harmonies, there was so much room to move. He found himself looking forward to the monsoons that year, would have wanted to hurry them along—except for Caidrun. . . .

Tamborel stood by the saraba, his palms pressed to the shutter, praying for Caidrun to come. The others were sound asleep, but he could not lie still. The wind was gusting outside, shaking the shutter, spraying it with pellets of rain: the monsoons had begun. He pictured the wide, dark sky beyond, and Caidrun lost under it. Even the lowliest stray creature was given shelter in this season. But Caidy, who would shelter her? He saw her lying beneath a hedge, her mouth filling with rain. He turned and leaned his head against the cold iron, feeling each jolt from the strident winds. Oh, why hadn't he gone to find her? Why had he listened to Silwender? "Caidrun will come," the High Zjarn said, every time he mentioned her. Now he couldn't go if he wanted to, couldn't get past the gate unseen. And if he did, where would he go, and how would he find her under the drenching rains?

Tamborel climbed onto his bunk and lay, falling at length into a restless sleep. A dream came, of wild, wet skies and empty plain, dark and wind-driven. Rain needles stung his flesh, his eyes; the wind pushed him back but he pressed on, driven by a sense of urgency. There, just ahead, a small smudge against the murky sky. "Caidy!"

The figure turned, flinging up its arms. A familiar voice wailed over the wind's whine. "Brel—where are you!"

Tamborel began to run, stumbled, fell headlong onto soggy turf. As he picked himself up, he saw her coming blindly toward him. "I'm here, Caidy—here!" On he ran, until he could see the rivulets streaming from her tangled locks and shining on her face. He'd almost reached her, arms outspread, when suddenly, she cried out. "Caidy, hold on!" he cried, but she melted like salt and was washed by the rains into the soggy turf.

Next morning, he lingered over breakfast, picking at his plate.

"Are you well?" Keiryn sat beside him at the empty table. "You're so very quiet."

"It's nothing." Tamborel stared down. The dream of Caidy frightened him, but he dared not share it, not even with Keiryn. Everyone here knew the tale of the boy who was turned to salt, and they dismissed it, together with all other such stories, as ignorant fancies. While Keiryn would likely not laugh at him, he'd find some other means to explain it away. "It's not surprising you had such a dream. It shows how worried you are about Caidrun."

Tamborel was certain there was more to it than that. He and Caidy had always been so close. He'd often sensed what she was feeling, even when they were apart. If she hurt or was in trouble, and if she needed him. Of course, since she had run away, that link had been broken. But his dream had been so *strong*. Was Caidy calling out to him? Was she in trouble somehow?

Keiryn guessed partway right, anyhow. "It's Caidrun, isn't it? You're afraid she's lost in the monsoons."

"Silwender said that she would turn up. So why

hasn't she? Something bad has happened, I just know it!"

"What does Silwender say now, with the monsoons here, and everything?"

Tamborel shook his head. "What can he say, but 'Try not to worry'?"

"I suppose." Keiryn sighed. "Tamborel, I'd be out of my mind, too. Listen, you have my ear any time."

In the weeks that followed, Tamborel found great comfort in Keiryn's offer, even though he didn't take it up. During the day, things did not seem so dire. Then, Tamborel imagined Caidrun with him in class, the two of them learning together. He could just see her blue eyes light up on hearing the wondrous harmonies, could see her perched beside him, chin in hands, listening while Perla intoned line on measured line from the Books of Lore.

Other times, he pictured Caidrun warm and dry beneath a friendly roof, an adopted member of some loving family, snug and sheltered from the driving rains. And why not? She could be charm itself when it so suited her.

But at night, as he lay listening to the rattle of iron shutter and the lash of rain against stone wall, Tamborel lay fearing for her safety, and slept badly, haunted by more dreams.

One day, in the middle of a class with Perla, he was startled to see one of her heynim suddenly leave her cluster and sink slowly to the floor. She bent and picked it up, holding it out for them all to see. "I have been expecting it. Look how it has lost its luster. It is the tenth heyn that I have lost this year." She broke off with a laugh. "Don't look so worried," she said. "I'll probably lose quite a few more to damp before the monsoons are over. But I'll soon replace them all, come spring."

"What do you do with your old ones, mistress?" asked Synla.

"For now, I keep them in a treasure box. At the end of the monsoons, we Fellows hold a ceremony to place them all in a vault below the main assembly hall, and"—Perla smiled regretfully—"I'm sorry, but students may not watch."

The monsoons dragged on, a dreary time that drained the spirits and slowed the keenest body down. Tamborel wondered how he ever could have liked the idea of being shut up in that place, away from outside light and air.

Then, just as tempers frayed to flash point, the wind changed, the rains eased, and the skies cleared. Men came to take the shutters down and fresh air blew through the open sarabas, sweeping out winter's must and mold. Folk began to liven up, looking to the mountains, watching out for heynim.

"Once Silwender gets his, he goes on spring tour," Hewl said. "No more tuning then, Tam-boy. Time to catch up on your reading and writing."

"He's doing well enough already," Keiryn said. "As well as you, Hewl."

"The first merchants' boys arrived today," said Jareyd. "Maybe tomorrow there'll be something for us."

"Merchants' boys?" Tamborel had not heard of those.

"Apprentices," Jareyd explained. "They travel with the grain and seed traders, spring and fall. They bring us packages and messages from home, for a modest fee. I'm hoping for some ginger candy from my grandmother."

"Nice," said Tamborel, wishing he might get something from home. Not that that was likely. He'd never noticed any such merchants' boys in Fahwyll. But to his astonishment, the very next day a youth came asking for him. He gave Tamborel a beautiful blue blanket from Eleyna and a pot of sun-bug honey. "She says to tell you Hwyllum's back is acting up again, but other than that all is well," the youth recited by rote. "There was a big to-do after you and Caidrun left the village. Four Pridicum men came for heynim and wouldn't leave until they were recompensed. Rufina and Bombrul, Yornwey and others each gave one heyn until the men's clusters were made good. The village was a-roil with the news of you in the Hon'faleyn. Some maintain it is a lie. Yornwey sends her respects and looks to see you home one day." The youth paused, checking off his fingers. "Let's see. Ah, yes. Tancey Bider is betrothed to Hormer Voor. And much as your mamma wants to see you, you'll understand a there is a lot to do in the fields now. She and Hwyllum will try to visit you as soon as they can."

Hormer Voor! thought Tamborel on his way to Perla's class. He was old enough to be Tancey's father!

Perla read again the passage from the First Book of Lore stating how the heynim came from over the Jagged Mountains and how it was forbidden to travel there. "Those who go beyond the peaks shall never have a heyn," the passage went on. Perla held up the tome, showing the margins filled with dire illustrations: tiny stricken figures, lying on the ground, all heynless. "What does that mean, do you think?"

"Sounds like a direct threat to me," said Hewl.

Perla smiled, her thinned-out cluster jingling. "Jareyd?"

"Could be. You definitely lose your heynim. Maybe you die as well."

"I see. Synla, what say you?" Synla was, by far, the best thinker in the class.

"If it's a threat, that implies some kind of vengeance, or punishment for wrongdoing," she said slowly.

Keiryn leaned forward. "Going to the Jagged Mountains is wrongdoing."

Synla smiled. "Or simply folly. This could be a prediction merely."

"*Prediction?*" Hewl clearly did not agree.

"You know: 'If you do this, that will follow.'" Synla nodded toward the saraba. "The prevailing winds blow this way, toward Minavar. So to snag a heyn, you stand this side of the ranges. Stand the other side, and the winds will carry the heynim away from you. That's plain common sense."

Hewl shook his head. "You can't say for sure it's not a threat."

"True." Synla nodded. "I'm simply offering another interpretation of the writings, Hewl."

"And a good one," Perla said. "Scholars have argued over these words for years. And likely will forever. Tamborel, do you agree with Synla?"

"I think so. They could be either a threat or a prediction—though I wouldn't care to put them to the test!"

Each day, Tamborel and Jareyd, Keiryn and Hewl looked out from their high vantage point, expecting at any moment to see bright heynim streaming toward them. But the skies remained empty. A week passed, two weeks, three, and folk began to grow restless. "They are late," Perla admitted. "I cannot recall this happening before. I cannot begin to guess why it would be."

The time for spring sowing arrived, and still the heynim had not come. Silwender canceled his tour amid reports of growing worry in the provinces. The mood in the Hon'faleyn went from sober to grim. At last, the High Zjarn convened the school: the students cramming the well of the assembly hall, the Fellows lining the galleries above. Tamborel scanned the Fellows for Rawl and Perla, marveling at the solid layer of swarms hovering above them. So many heynim still, despite the hundreds that they'd buried only weeks before!

Silwender climbed onto the platform in front of the hall and raised his arms. In the sudden hush, the High Zjarn's thin dry voice carried to the rafters. "Since rumor is rife, I deem it best to speak plain: the heynim swarms do not come yet this year, no one can say why. Yet we must be calm, watch, and wait. Above all, say nothing beyond these walls of the danger's extent. Talk changes nothing, and only sows fear."

Lessons resumed in an air of suppressed excitement, the sort that comes when great disaster looms. Peril charged the air, magnifying every look and gesture. And when Tamborel caught his fellow students' eyes, he saw his own concern reflected there: if the heynim never came, *what would happen to their world?*

•21•

Later that day, Tamborel went for his lesson with Silwender. "You look anxious, boy," the High Zjarn said. "And it's not surprising. It's hard on you young ones, away from home. I'll have the tutors speak with you all later, to hear your concerns about your families."

About Caidy, too, thought Tamborel. Who would counsel her if things got worse? His worry went up another notch.

Silwender sent a cluster over to him. "Come. We have work to do, in fact it's more important than ever to keep our mind on it. Begin."

Tamborel spun a faleyn in rising quarter tones, a purely mechanical exercise supposedly. But as he bent his mind to it, anxiety stole in, distorting the purity of the intervals. When Tamborel had done, the High Zjarn stayed silent for a while. "Mmmm," he said eventually. "Even I, who have come to bear with indifference the worst that the world can heap upon me, feel your faleyn's pull. Yes, I own you've made me anxious." Silwender drew the heynim back into his swarm. "It's a singular gift, young man, to tune what's within you, and sound its echo in another's heart. I confess you do confound me. I'd pegged you for a future zjarn."

Tamborel leaned forward. "And now?"

Silwender shook his head. "The zjarn tunes faleyn to the physical body. I've done it best and longest of anyone alive. That's why I'm High Zjarn, head of the Hon'faleyn. But as for you . . ." The old man spread his hands.

"Could I be a Spinner?" The moment it was out, Tamborel felt foolish. All this talk of zjarn and Spinner and he heynless!

Silwender frowned. "I . . . cannot say."

"Because I have no cluster?"

Silwender smiled. "That we'll remedy. Tamborel, your gift is so special it has as yet no name. It needs careful thought."

Tamborel looked away, feeling hollow. Silwender thought it special? It wasn't, not at all. "What you just said about my sensing how folk feel? Rawl calls it the power of empathy—and Keiryn has it, too."

182

"Hmmm." Silwender stroked his beard. "Empathy is the power to *identify with* another's feelings—feelings that are manifest. Yes, your friend Keiryn does have that worthy gift. But you, Tamborel, you prick us in unexpected places, stirring within us feelings we don't even know we have." Silwender put his hand over his heart and beat a light tattoo with his fingers. "As I said, I think you find them first within yourself, then spin them into faleyn which find resonance in us. During these past months, you've made me feel joy of which I'd never dream myself capable. And pain so unbearable it has long been buried and forgot."

"Oh. Forgive me, master."

Silwender waved away his apology. "Rather I should thank you, boy. This will prove a wondrous tool. Perhaps you'll cure what I cannot."

"But you can cure anyone of anything, sir."

Silwender shook his head. "I treat sickness that is manifest. I cannot heal the undiscovered ill—such as that which afflicts you, Tamborel. No one can. The only hope is first to find it out—and perhaps this gift of yours will help us do that."

"And Caidrun? Might it help her too?"

"Always we come back to Caidrun." The High Zjarn looked wry. "Well, let Caidrun come, and let us speak with her, and then we'll see."

"I sometimes wish—"

"Wish what?"

"That I'd gone on to find her."

"And I say again where would you have gone, eh, boy? And what if you'd gone wandering while she turned up here? No, you're in the proper place, of that I'm sure."

Silwender was so sure of everything, thought Tamborel, shaking out his new blanket and spreading it over his bunk. About this so-called gift of his, and about Caidy coming to the Hon'faleyn. He himself was not so convinced about either. He exchanged good-nights and climbed into bed. While he could not deny he had a way of tuning faleyn better than most, if there were more to it as Silwender said, wouldn't he just *know* it? And all that business about it promising to prove a wondrous tool when he couldn't snag a single heyn! On the other hand, if he did possess this power, how wonderful if he could use it on Caidy. All those years of torment, while he could offer only sympathy. Though that had helped her, some, when she had nothing else. He lay on his back, closed his eyes.

Where are you, Caidy? What are you doing now?

Tamborel turned onto his side. How had she vanished so completely? At first, he'd been relieved as reports of her ceased. But now he found himself wishing for more such, for any sign that she was still alive.

When at last sleep came, it was troubled. He

dreamed they sat together by the minnow brook, dabbling their toes in the water. The air was warm, the sky was blue, and Caidrun was smiling.

"Poor Brel. Brel the Heynless. Never mind, take my cluster. I don't want it, I have no ear." She sent it toward him.

"Caidy, don't. It's yours. Besides, I don't deserve it."

"Oh, but you do, catch!" The heynim gathered speed, golden pellets shooting with deadly force toward him.

"*Caidy!*" Tamborel sat bolt upright in his bed, his chest heaving, his face slick with sweat. Had he cried aloud? He listened, heard the steady breathing around him. He slumped over, wiping his face on his nightshirt. Those heynim coming at him like slingshot! "Catch," Caidy had said, her tone pure venom. Oh, how could she!

It was only a dream, Tamborel reassured himself. Even so, it still hurt. He lay down again and closed his eyes, trying to find his way back to the minnow brook, but the sunny day had turned to night and the mild air to a howling wind, no sign of Caidy. "Caidy!" Her mocking laugh came back in answer. Tamborel made toward the sound, glimpsed her shadowy shape ahead. "Caidy—wait!" Behind her rose a line of ragged peaks. As he raced to catch her, pale mist writhed up from the ground and coiled around her. Caidy spread her arms and spun around, her skirts swirling. Then she slowly sank from sight. Tamborel stumbled forward, fetching up before a jagged hole with steps leading down. He knelt, and leaned into the hole, cupping his hands to shout. A puff of cold damp air rose toward him, rank with mold and decay. Tamborel's skin went icy. *"Caidy!"* The echoes resounded far below. Her shrill laugh faintly answered, then all was silence. As he straightened, mist rose from the ground and curled toward him. Tamborel leaped up and turned to flee.

He awoke in a shivery sweat so bad that they sent for Silwender.

"Hmm. A touch of the moldy fever. Odd that you should get it now, so long after the monsoons. Well, whatever its cause, I give it two days—though you'll be keeping to your bed for at least a full week more."

As Silwender said, it took only two days for the heat and pain of the fever to subside. But Tamborel lay for another week, locked within its aftermath— and in his nightmare's thrall. Once, when he and Keiryn were alone, he almost told about the horror still palpable within him. But somehow, he couldn't bring himself to give it voice, not even though Keiryn practically invited him to speak up. "It's not just the fever, is it?" Keiryn had come back to the chamber midmorning for a warmer tunic, ostensibly. He perched on the opposite bunk. "If you'd care to share, I'd be glad to listen. You can count on me, you know, and I'd never tell anyone."

186

Of his three roommates, Keiryn would be the one to confide in, of that Tamborel was sure. While he enjoyed parrying with Hewl, and while Jareyd was unquestionably their leader in matters of rules and protocol, Keiryn was most like the brother Tamborel had never had. "I'm fine, really I am," Tamborel answered. "But if I'm ever in a bad fix, I'll call on you, I promise."

"Snap out of it, Tam-boy," Hewl said, into the second week. "At this rate, you'll still be abed feeling sorry for yourself when we're all graybeards." Hewl's barb proved more effective than all the sympathy. Three days after, Tamborel was headed back to class.

"So you decided to live," Silwender remarked, when Tamborel went for his lesson. "You took your time, though. The fever lasted just two days. But, then," he went on, as Tamborel began to protest, "it was the affliction of the spirit you found hard to fight. Care to tell me its cause?"

Tamborel hesitated. "I had a nightmare," he said at last, watching Silwender's face. But the old man only nodded, looking grave. "Go on."

It was hard at first, but as Tamborel spilled the horror from his mind, he began to feel relief. When he had done, Silwender surveyed him from under his brows. "What do *you* make of your nightmare, Tamborel?"

"I'm not sure, sir. Bits and pieces of it really happened. Caidy and I sat by the brook just before she

ran away, that was when she let me tune her cluster." Tamborel shivered. "Those heynim coming at
me—that happened, too, though that I don't remember. It's how I had my accident, you see. How the bad
things started. But Caidy was only two and didn't
know what she was doing." He winced, recalling her
deliberate cruelty. "That got twisted up in my dream.
She'd never hurt me on purpose, I swear."

"Hmmm. Have you had other dreams like this?"

Tamborel thought back. "Yes, though not lately."

"Tell me about them."

Tamborel recounted his earlier dreams: of Caidy in
the rain and dark, lost, or melting like salt into the
ground.

"I see. Well, let me think, then we'll talk some
more. Maybe these dreams will help our search."

"To find where Caidy is?"

Silwender sighed. "To find where you are, boy.
Now to other matters. About this gift of yours: I am
calling it *the power of resonance*. And if one day you
hold a swarm, you'll be our first *Spinner of the
Resonances*."

Tamborel stared. "I don't know what to say."

"For that I am glad. I'm not giving out largesse,
only a name for your power, and a title should you
ever come to wield it. But much must happen before
that. Now: say nothing of this to anyone, do you
hear?"

Spinner of the Resonances. Tamborel repeated the

188

title over and over, savoring its sound. For a while back in class, he sat straight and held his head high. Spinner of the Resonances sounded so much better than Tamborel the Heynless! But as the day wore on, the euphoria wore off, giving way to older doubt and worry. *It's a singular gift, young man, to tune what's within you, and sound its echo in another's heart.* Silwender expected something of him, something that he was sure wasn't there. He had nothing: no gift, no heynim. Just a lot of expectations. And a heap of worry over Caidy. What was he doing in that place? he asked himself irritably.

By bedtime, Tamborel was in a dangerous mood.

"You look so tired," Keiryn said. "Are you all right?"

"Don't fuss, he's well enough," Jareyd said, climbing into his bunk.

"He was more than well when he left Silwender," Hewl said. "Did you notice him come into class? What did the old man say, Tam-boy? Did he make you a Fellow? Or tell you something of your girl friend? Come on, spill."

Normally, Tamborel would have thrown out some friendly retort, but tonight he found their harmless banter unbearable. Without a word or look, Tamborel got into bed and lay, facing the wall. There was a short, awkward silence. Then someone turned out the light. Tamborel lay stiffly, willing himself asleep. Before he was even halfway, the nightmare images

189

sprang into his mind as if they'd been lying in wait: of the converging heynim, of Caidrun dancing with the mist wraiths then vanishing underground. He shuddered, shrinking down into the bedclothes. He could have told his roommates, and they'd have laughed him out of taking an old folktale to heart. But the fact remained that as he lay there in the dark and on the edge of sleep his fear was almost too real to bear: *what if Caidy had danced with the mist wraiths and they had made her theirs?*

Part Four

•22•

Next day, loud bells clanged, rousting everyone from bed in great excitement. "Heynim!" Jareyd cried. "At last!"

The excitement was short-lived. The heynim, barely one hundred in all, drifted in twos and threes high above the city rooftops. These went to the Fellows in the Hon'faleyn: not near enough to go around. In the weeks that followed, though sentinels kept close sky watch, no more were sighted.

Tamborel noticed a marked shift in the atmosphere. The winter had taken a greater toll on heynim than usual. The deeper tones especially had thinned out, and the rich level of sound was noticeably diminished.

So was their power. Although the Sky Spinners toiled around the clock with their depleted swarms, spring appeared to stall. The sun shone pale without any warmth, windstorms killed off many newborn grazing beasts, and frosts nipped the new and tender shoots of grain.

Silwender canceled any tour of the provinces until further notice. *Charity begins at home. Our gate is swamped with local folk.* It seemed not only Tamborel had taken the moldy fever out of season. Townsfolk also ailing from swollen joints, coughs, and wheezes trekked through the public healing halls in endless lines. At last, the numbers grew so great that the novices were called in to assist with simple chores: taking names, heating poultices, giving remedies to sip. At night, the zjarns rode out on qarlim to tend folk prostrated with the moldy fever—the moldy fever—still at this late date!

The Fellows being now too busy tending the sick to teach, classes were suspended. The students were set to work alone in the library, studying subjects of their own choosing.

Tamborel took down several books on spinning faleyn; fat books compiled by the Fellows over the years. So many words, he thought. So much—stuff—on something simple as breathing! But as he browsed through, he began to see that there was more to spinning than he'd thought, and that the Fellows had acquired a special know-how that came only after years

194

of practice. By the end of one morning, he was all too grateful that they'd troubled to record their hard-won mysteries for him to share.

"I see you've put your time to good use," Silwender said, at Tamborel's next lesson. "Your skills have increased tenfold."

Spring dragged into summer, barely. The skies stayed weak and rain fell every day. What crops survived were poor and blighted.

Harvest came—and went.

"It's a crying shame," Hewl grumbled. "We'd been so looking forward to the Harvest Festival." A three-day gala when folk brought tributes by the cartload to the Hon'faleyn and the city was one huge open house. When the novices decked themselves in colorful hoods and gowns and ran the streets to be showered with food and drink to celebrate the end of their first year. "Ah, well. I'll have to mark it somehow. I think I'll grow a beard."

"A beard!"

"Don't look so shocked, Tam-boy. I'm almost twenty-one."

Come to think, Tamborel himself was going on nineteen now. A fact he'd hardly noticed with no one to remind him.

"How can you talk of galas and beards when folk can scarcely feed themselves?" Jareyd demanded. "It's going to be a hard winter out there."

"Never mind about out there," Hewl said. "It's going to be short rations all around. I heard today there'll be no novices this year—there's barely enough food for us."

The skies darkened. The monsoons came early and with a vengeance.

In the Hon'faleyn, the mood was grim.

"They tell us to keep a good face on things," Hewl grumbled. "I've clean forgotten what it's like not to feel a growl in my belly."

"Me, too," Jareyd agreed. "I'm counting the days to spring."

"Then the lines of sick will come again," said Keiryn.

Tamborel found his sessions with Silwender sorely taxing. Not that he found tuning difficult. In fact, he now could handle some sixty or so heynim at one time. The trouble was that worry touched his every faleyn, however hard he tried to keep it out. Like the one he was tuning now, an elementary Sky Spinner's exercise. "Tamborel, I asked for *all* shades of blue. I hear only pale gray. Where are the deep blue tones of summer? You're not a novice any longer: *concentrate!*"

"I cannot hold the deep tones steady. The winter's been too long."

"That's your excuse?" Silwender's tone was sharp. "What if our Sky Spinners thought that way, eh? Day and night they tune their faleyn to the deepest, purest blues. No matter that they have lost half their

196

heynim. Or that the monsoons have not ended. No matter that the rains still come down. That's *discipline*, Tamborel. It's what remains when all else fails."

"But, master," Tamborel began. Oh, what was the use? He let the faleyn go. "What is going to happen?"

The High Zjarn clasped his hands together in his lap. "I do not know."

The next day, the Fellows suspended lessons as they had the year before, dismissing Tamborel's class into the library. At first, he leafed through the now-familiar books on spinning, but growing restless, he got up and wandered from the main chamber into the little dusty rooms beyond where lesscommonly read books were stored. He scanned the shelves idly, took down a heavy brass-bound tome, opened the catch, and lifted back the wooden cover. *Myth and Legend of Alyafaleyn:* the title was all but gone. He turned the brittle pages carefully, until, suddenly, he froze. Tiny figures like wisps of vapor with demon faces danced in the margins: mist wraiths! Tamborel took the book to a nearby table and began to read the text. "Some versions of the myth state that the wraiths dance at the *edge* of the world, while others say *end*," a note explained. "But all versions agree that the edge or end in question is the Jagged Mountain range. One of the earliest versions of the myth speaks of a mortal dancing *at our world's end*. This gave rise to the popular belief that if a mortal should ever dance with the mist wraiths, it would somehow bring about the ruination of our world. This in turn gave rise to the ancient law (still in force) that forbids all travel to those desolate peaks."

Tamborel slammed down the book and fled.

That night, he could not sleep. His nightmares had subsided over the months. Sometimes he'd gotten so absorbed in books and tuning with Silwender that he'd gone days scarcely thinking of Caidrun at all. Then, his thoughts of Caidrun dancing with the mist wraiths seemed less real, his fear unfounded. But now, with so many sick and in need . . .

Tamborel sat up, hugging his knees. Since Caidrun had vanished, the whole world had gone awry, and fair skies were but a memory. Virtually the last time he'd enjoyed such was on that last evening with Caidy by the minnow brook. Such a peaceful time that had been, and full of promise.

They had burned the hateful helmet and he had tuned his first faleyn.

Of course, Caidy, not content to just savor the moment, had picked things apart, arguing as to what the heynim were and where they came from. She'd actually talked of tracing them back to their source.

It's a thought . . .

An ingenious one, from the finest mind in Fahwyll. . . .

Tamborel froze, remembering the book he'd read that morning.

198

. . . if a mortal should ever dance with the mist wraiths, it would somehow bring about the ruination of our world.

He thought of Caidy vanishing. Of her threats: *I'll show all of you who Caidy really is, just wait and see.* Everything was dying. Soon they would not know what was the season, or even whether it was day or night.

The ruination of our world!

"Oh, Caidy, what has happened to you! What have you done!" Tamborel slipped from his bunk and, throwing his blanket about his shoulders, went to sit in the passage outside.

It was unthinkable.

But he had thought it.

Tamborel sat, staring at the floor until a light tap on his shoulder started him up. "I can't sleep either." Keiryn sat down alongside, hugging himself against the chill. "What's wrong?"

"I cannot say." Tamborel shivered.

"It's Caidrun, isn't it? Is it very bad?" Tamborel nodded.

"Is she . . . dead?"

Tamborel hesitated. He'd nursed his fears so long. But this was too much to bear alone—and he dared not tell Silwender. Perhaps if he shared his fear with Keiryn, it would shrink in the telling. "It's just about as bad as that. But if I say what it is, you must promise not to tell." Of course, Keiryn knew hardly anything, so Tamborel started from the beginning, from Silwender's visit to Fahwyll before Caidrun was born, right up to the evening at the brook. Without pause, he described the fight at the well, and how he'd betrayed Caidrun by doing absolutely nothing.

Keiryn shook his head. "I can't believe they'd treat a baby so harshly. Not that I blame you," he added hastily. "You were too small yourself to stop them. And you did what you could."

"But I joined them in the end," Tamborel said bitterly. "I let things ride. I didn't stick by her—me, her one true friend."

"Tamborel, I'm sorry. But she didn't exactly give you time to make amends. Don't be so hard on yourself: you came all this way to find her. It's no use telling you not to worry, but didn't you say how sharp and tough she was? I'll bet she's safe somewhere, and still at odds with everyone."

Tamborel shivered now. "That is not what's keeping me awake, Keiryn."

"Then what?"

"I think she's done what she said she'd do down by the brook: I think she went to seek the heynim's source."

"You mean she traveled to the Jagged Mountains? But it's forbidden!"

"That wouldn't stop Caidy." Tamborel jumped up. "Keiryn, I have to go after her."

"But you can't." Keiryn looked at him closely now. "Oh, Tamborel. There'll be such trouble. And danger,

200

too. Look, why don't you just wait till the monsoons end?"

"Because," Tamborel said slowly. "They won't end, Keiryn. Spring will never come at this rate, and neither will she. Because . . . I think—" He stopped, then pressed on again firmly. "I think the two are connected. I think she not only went to seek the heynim's source. I think she found it. I believe that Caidy is mixed up in all our troubles."

"You can't be serious—yes, yes, I see you are." Keiryn whistled. "All that fuss about her scattering other people's clusters—she does sound precocious. But—you're not suggesting she's the reason why the new ones haven't come these past two years?"

It did sound preposterous, put so plain. But, then, Keiryn did not know Caidy. "The more we speak of it, the surer I feel it in my bones. I have to go, I know it now. Promise me again that you won't tell?"

Keiryn shivered. "It's so *cold*! You'll not get out of Minavar on foot in these rains." He leaned forward, his arms tight-wrapped around his ribs. "Unless I go too."

"No!" Tamborel said sharply. Then added more mildly, "Why?"

"I've ridden qarlim all my life. We'll borrow one and—"

"No." Tamborel raised a hand. "You asked to *hear* my trouble, Keiryn. Not to bear it."

Keiryn almost smiled. "But you don't ride, and

201

you'll go nowhere on foot. A qarl can take us wherever you want to go, even in the rains."

"But I go to the *Jagged Mountains*."

Fear flickered in Keiryn's eyes. "Then so do I."

Tamborel pointed. "What about your heynim out in the rains?"

"I'd stow them in a bag. That's what the zjarns do right now when they go out to tend the sick. And as for riding to the Jagged Mountains: let's say I'll go as far as I am able."

Tamborel shook his head. "What if you stopped halfway? There'd be no turning back for me. So how would you survive out there alone? And how would you get back here without a beast?"

Keiryn shrugged. "Where I come from they say you cross a brook one stone at a time. Let's get started."

From then on, they ate sparingly, saving what they could, stowing scraps of dried fruit, hardtack and biscuit under their mattresses. Keiryn stole out to the stables and earmarked a sturdy beast. Then one afternoon, about a week after their talk, they stepped unnoticed from the crowded healing hall. While Tamborel packed their gear, Keiryn stored his heynim. Wrapped against the elements, they strode boldly to the stables. No one questioned them as Keiryn fitted a double saddle to the qarl and led the beast across the outer courtyard. "We go on an errand of mercy," said Tamborel, striving to sound calm. Old Kowl the gatekeeper let them through with grunt and a nod and scuttled back into the shelter of his booth.

Heads down, bodies bent into the driving rain, Tamborel and Keiryn passed through the gate and down into the streets of Minavar.

·23·

After only a couple of hours, it got too dark to travel farther. Slipping from the qarl's back, they huddled under a makeshift shelter—their capes tied together—and nibbled at their rations. "I'm surprised to find a road out here," Tamborel remarked. He'd pictured the plain totally devoid of traffic, save perhaps for wild beasts.

"There are settlements on the plains," Keiryn told him. "So I suppose the merchants need some kind of road to take supplies. We should be glad, for it will make our ride easier."

"How far does it run, do you know?"

"To the last settlement, let's hope. World's End,

they call it. It's about a day's ride from the ranges. How do you feel, Tamborel?"

Tamborel's rear was tender from the saddle, and his knees were stiff and sore. He shifted painfully. "Just fine. But it's the strangest thing: now we're on our way, I feel better." Even though the wind blew chill under their shelter, and the rain trickled down his back.

Keiryn took a drink from the water bottle, handed it across. "It's because you feel at last you're doing something, probably. You've been getting more and more frustrated shut up in the Hon'faleyn this past year and some. Not all the time, but I've seen it come in gusts."

That was true. Trust Keiryn to have noticed. Just beyond, the qarl shifted, seeking longer grass. Tamborel marveled that it could make itself so comfortable out in such bleak weather. "This place is no place even for a beast. You must be wishing you'd stayed behind already, Keiryn."

"It crossed my mind an hour or so back. But I'm really glad I came."

"You can't be serious."

"Oh, it's true. For one thing, I'd never have been able to sleep nights, if I'd let you come alone. For another, I've never done anything daring before. My folk kept me on a tight rein, you know? They said my constitution wasn't strong."

"And they sent you to become a *zjarn*?" Zjarns had

to be strong to risk the open road, and to endure in all kinds of places.

"Silwender's a zjarn, and see how fragile he looks."

Tamborel grinned. "We all know differently. But coming with me took a different kind of strength, Keiryn."

"Don't I know it?" Keiryn laughed dryly. "I confess I'm in two minds, still. Remember the discussion we had about the passage in the Lore Book, whether it was a threat or a prediction? 'Those who go beyond the peaks shall never have a heyn.' The thought of going even near them scares me."

"You can turn back, you know. It's not too late."

"No?" Keiryn retorted. "At this point, I'd rather scale the highest peak than face Silwender."

It took two days to reach Westerly, their first sign of human life since quitting Minavar. Almost halfway to the foothills, the settlement was about the size of Pridicum, only rougher and run-down. The qarl slipped and slid the length of the rain-lashed street, in one end and out the other. No one saw them: who would, through those tight, dark shutters? His bones and muscles aching from long hours in the saddle, his raw, chafed skin afire, Tamborel rode behind Keiryn, head down, while water poured off his hood, cascading down his back. They spoke little, for to turn or tilt one's head risked a dousing. But Tamborel was grateful for his friend's presence. And the gesture had moved

206

him deeply. Who else would have left the Hon'faleyn to risk this road and certain censure on return?

They pressed on over sodden plain. Where the road dipped, the water was so deep it nearly reached the qarl's high barrel belly. And visibility was never more than a few paces in all directions. "How does the beast know where to tread?" Tamborel called in Keiryn's ear.

Keiryn leaned back. "By instinct. And don't let those spindly legs fool you. It could walk up a wall."

They pressed on, the rains unceasing, the skies getting darker, until at last they reached World's End. With each step now, Tamborel's desire to reach the mountains grew stronger. Caidy had made this journey on foot, propelled by her anger and bitterness. How she must have hated him. He made a little moaning sound in his throat. *I'm coming, Caidy. I'm coming.*

Keiryn called over his shoulder. "Miserable place. To think that people live behind those walls."

Tamborel glanced around. The shacks were scarcely visible behind thick sheets of rain.

The end of the world.

The end of the road, at least. Tamborel peered ahead, shivering convulsively. But they had his instinct to guide them still—a needle to a magnet that grew stronger with every step.

Keiryn reined in the qarl. "One more day, Tamborel. And only half that to reach the first foothills." He sounded nervous.

Tamborel felt nervous, too. Scared and excited, both at once. He nodded back toward the shacks. "You can stop here, if you like."

"Never," Keiryn said. He nudged the qarl along.

Around midday, the ground began to rise. All at once, Tamborel felt a wave of energy flash through him. From somewhere deep inside, a strange, familiar tingling surged, breaking out onto his skin. Then, as suddenly, the sensation passed. Tamborel leaned forward, rubbing his arms. "Did you feel that?" he shouted, into the wind.

"Feel what?"

Tamborel opened his mouth, closed it again. Chimes, he'd swear. He swallowed his excitement, reluctant now to share it.

Keiryn slued around. "Let's stop. Rest up for our last leg."

Stop? Tamborel could push on now all day and night!

Their eyes met. "If you want," Tamborel began. *If you want to back out now, I will not blame you,* he meant to say, but quit. If and when Keiryn's nerve finally deserted him, he would confess it in his own good time. "If you want," he repeated, checking his impatience.

Keiryn looked relieved. They went on a little farther, watching for the meager shelter of bush or tree. "See: over there." Keiryn pointed left. Off the track a short way loomed a smudgy mass, a ramshackle cottage. On the doorstep lay a man, the rain bouncing off his back in pellets. They scrambled down and ran. Keiryn knelt and put his hand to the man's brow. "He has the moldy fever." They carried him inside between them and laid him on a cot beside the fireplace. Tamborel straightened, breathing through his mouth. The air was foul. The place was squalid, with leaky roof and sooty walls but, glory, glowing embers in the hearth! While Tamborel stirred the ashes and threw on wet wood, Keiryn stripped the man of his wet clothes and tucked the covers over him. "There, that's better. Look, Tamborel. His heynim." He shook a kerchief loose, and out popped four intyl. Their shine was almost gone, their chiming barely audible. Freed, they sank down to hover by the man's head. "In their last hours, by the look of it. And so is he, if we don't do something. Tamborel, we must go back for help."

"To World's End? We'll lose a whole day!" The log began to smolder, filling the room with smoke. In a spasm of coughing, Tamborel knelt and blew on the log, coaxing up a meager flame.

"Tamborel, he badly needs a zjarn."

"Can you see one living in that hole? We'll tend to him ourselves."

"How? We don't tune faleyn yet—" Keiryn broke off, then exclaimed eagerly. "*You!* You know how. You can use my cluster." He patted the bag at his belt.

What could Tamborel say? The faleyn that he

tuned were not for sickness of the flesh. But Keiryn did not know that, for Silwender had forbidden him to tell. Keiryn assumed with all the rest that he practiced to be a regular zjarn. Oh, what to do? "I'll try."

Keiryn unhitched his bag, shook out his heynim into the room, pulled them in to hover between them. Tamborel knew the cluster well, and the nature of each heyn. Where to start? Tamborel thought back to his last bout with the moldy fever, how clean and cool and soothing Silwender's chimes had felt. He closed his eyes and set to work.

"He's cooler. You did it, Tamborel." Keiryn stood and stretched. Gray light filtered through cracks in the ceiling, picking out the grimy contents of the shack. A table, a chair. Two lamps. Some pots that had not been washed in an age. The man stirred and groaned. "What now?" Keiryn said.

Indeed. All night, Tamborel had thought of Caidy. Of how close they were and how soon they would be face to face. Now this. He wanted to pick up and be gone. Why, they might reach the ranges by midday. But how could they leave at this point? The moldy fever had a nasty habit of returning. To run out now would be wrong. "He needs broth."

They found a food locker—an old crate—beside the door. In it was dry bread, a heap of sour butter, and a lump of greasy cheese. And some wrinkled roots

210

gone soft. Tamborel laid the vegetables on the table: not much to work with. "He won't need a zjarn now, but he still needs tending."

"It will take only one." Keiryn found a paring knife, began to scrape a root, exposing bright orange flesh. "I'll stay. You go—now. Be quick, you're wasting daylight."

Tamborel could scarcely mask his eagerness. "You're sure?"

Keiryn was sure, all right. In fact, he seemed relieved. "Hurry back. I hope your Caidrun is as light as you say, or we'll have to take turns walking back to Minavar."

Tamborel slung on his cloak and looked around the room. Now, at the last minute, he felt guilty. "Here, I'll bring in more wood before I go." He scrabbled around in the yard, carried in armfuls of blackened logs and stacked them on the hearth where they began to steam at once. Then he gathered up his things, went to the door and opened it a little way, letting in a slice of wind and rain. Impulsively, he strode inside and gave Keiryn a quick, farewell hug. "Thank you. You're my best friend, next to Caidy. Stay warm and dry. I'll try not to be too long."

"Remember how to call the qarl?" Keiryn followed him to the door. Tamborel cupped his hands and shouted. "Co . . . me! Co . . . me!" The beast teetered up out of the water curtain, leaves poking from its muzzle, its jaws working. "Kneel!" The qarl obeyed,

Tamborel mounted. "Don't forget to hobble him when you stop to rest, or he'll wander!" Keiryn called from the open doorway.

"For mercy's sake, get inside!" Tamborel yelled, waving him back. Keiryn saluted in farewell, then finally closed the door.

Tamborel nudged the beast on, up the slopes, Keiryn forgotten already. He gazed up into the thick gray sky. Back in the Hon'faleyn—when they could still be seen—the foothills had looked soft and round as cushions. At close quarters, they were covered in tussocks of wiry grass lumpy as cobbles and pocked with sharp gray stones.

The way grew steeper, yet the qarl, with its unerring nose for safety, managed to find the easiest way, a narrow trail—a dried-up stream bed, probably—that cut over and around the slopes, marking the path of least resistance. And probably the longest one, too, Tamborel thought ungratefully. Four hours, and they hadn't yet made the first big rise.

As they climbed, the driving rains eased, and fine droplets of moisture hung in the air, drifting like curtains in the wind. A little farther on, Tamborel began to sense the chimes again. No burst of energy this time, but a faint, all-over pricking, the sort he'd felt all those years before when watching Silwender's approach along the Pridicum road.

Almost there, Caidy. Could she tell?

The way grew steeper and trickier. While he

couldn't see them through the rainy mist, Tamborel knew the peaks were looming over them, and that this was a foretaste of what was to come. From his high chamber in the Hon'faleyn, the ranges had seemed ethereal, a mysterious deepening of the sky. And here was the reality: treacherous rock slope that had even the sure-footed qarl stumbling about. He urged the beast on over a low spur, only to fetch up, sharp, on a chasm's brink. Off to the left, a narrow ridge of rock arched like a rainbow to the chasm's far side. He slid down off the qarl's back and leaned out over the chasm's edge. Misty rain fell away down, no sign of the bottom. Tamborel swallowed. *Oh, Caidy.*

Closer to, Tamborel found the surface of that natural stone span was round, not flat; that it was less like a bridge, more like the fossilized rib of some ancient, monstrous beast long since swallowed by the chasm. . . .

Pulling himself together, Tamborel took the qarl's bridle and edged toward the narrow span. The qarl, endowed with natural good sense, resolved to go in the opposite direction. There followed an epic tug-of-war until, in the end, the beast's training prevailed and Tamborel managed to drag it across by main force.

By the time they were over, Tamborel's knees were weak, and he was drenched in sweat. He mopped his face, looking around. It was getting dark. But he didn't want to stop that close to such a treacherous drop, so he remounted and moved on. By the time they crested the first big rise, it was so dark that the qarl tripped, almost tumbling them down the other side. Tamborel dismounted and led the beast on to a stretch of leveler ground. There he sat, huddled in his cape and missing Keiryn. He nibbled on a crust, took a swig of water, then, utterly exhausted, keeled over and fell asleep.

It was just dawn when Tamborel awoke. "Though you can hardly tell," he declared loudly. The sky was dark, the air thick with mist and rain, just as in his nightmares. No sign of the qarl. "Co . . . me!" There was no response. Of course. He hadn't hobbled it. Don't forget, Keiryn had warned him. Or it will walk. Tamborel began to cast around, peering through the murk, calling "Come!" in growing exasperation. All at once, he halted.

There was something familiar about this place; the lie of the turf, the small rocks jutting out. He whirled about in alarm. Nothing. A shiver went up his back, as, all at once, he had the feeling that someone watched him. He turned again, and this time, cried out. A column of mist had risen from the turf and was floating toward him.

A mist wraith!

He made to flee, then checked and fearfully stood his ground. *"Caidy?"*

The column writhed and twisted, dancing toward

him. Another moment, and they'd touch, thought Tamborel, powerless to move. But as he made to close his eyes, the column spiraled up and vanished on the wind.

As Tamborel stood, his heart jumping, his breath coming tight and fast, new forms rose from the same spot and coiled toward him. As in a dream, he advanced to that place, then halted, feeling an icy draft:

At his feet, a ragged hole and steps leading down.

·24·

Tamborel leaned over, peering into the depths. His dream—exactly! The steps fell steeply, vanishing into the dark. Deep-cut and narrow, they were worn concave in the middle from much use. They were also in great disrepair: cracked and crumbling at the edges. Clearly they had not been used in ages.

Swinging his legs over the edge of the hole, Tamborel tested the top step. It wobbled slightly, but held. He started on down, step by careful step. As he went, the tingling in his skin grew stronger.

Caidy was down there, he just knew it. Caidy—and the chimes!

Six steps down the light was gone. He glanced back

216

up, blinking at the falling mist. The sky was a ragged gray patch, small and far away. Six more steps, and even that was gone. Tamborel put a hand to his chest, feeling stifled suddenly, as he had at times in the shuttered Hon'faleyn. He fought the urge to scramble back up to the surface, and the panicky thoughts flashing through his mind. What was he thinking of! What if the steps caved in? What if he lost his footing and toppled down—how far would he fall? He closed his eyes and, shutting out his fears, focused instead upon Caidy. He breathed the rank, dank mix of stone and mold, slowly, deliberately, in and out, until he felt his spirit rising. Then he carried on.

As he went deeper, excitement, not panic broke his careful calm. Any moment now he and Caidy would come face to face! He could almost feel Caidy throw herself upon him: "Oh, Brel! I thought you'd never come!"

The air grew more chill, and rank. Yet the deeper he went, the higher his energy surged. Icy air beaded on his cloak, yet inside it he began to feel hot. Steps gave way to tunnel floor sloping gently down. Tamborel picked up pace until, all at once, he ran blind smack into . . . a wall? He groped about, traced rusty hinges. And at the other edge, a massive ring: the latch. Not a wall: a door, heavy as a monsoon door only made of wood.

He raised the latch, tried to turn it, but it wouldn't budge.

217

Stooping, Tamborel found a little hole. He put his mouth to the hole and called. "Hall—oo—hoo!" His shout rang up the passage.

The echoes faded. Deep silence.

He bent again, and put his ear to the hole. A moment later, he exclaimed softly. *Chimes?* He held quite still, not breathing, fixed on the space behind the door. Yes, chimes. Faint—not faraway. *Muffled.*

Chimes!

Tamborel called through the keyhole. "Hall . . . oooo!" Then he held his breath, straining to hear. Quiet, then, all at once, a rush of chimes as though another, farther, door had opened then closed on them again. Feet crunched over stone, closer, closer. Someone was coming!

A bolt slid back. Tamborel braced himself.

The door creaked open, torch light flickered in the widening gap.

A pause, then the door swung wide. On the open threshold stood a slight figure draped in shawl and long, ragged skirts. One small hand gripped the door catch, the other held a torch aloft. Tamborel blinked and looked again: a thick mop of dark, bushy hair shadowed the stark white face. "Caidy!"

For one heartbeat, Caidrun stood, looking up at him, lips parted, eyes wide with shock. Tamborel's heart leapt, catching something else. She *was* glad to see him, overjoyed, in fact! He took a step, reaching

218

for her hand. At that—it all happened so fast—she shoved the torch at him, grabbed the door, and began hauling it shut.

"Caidy—no!" Tamborel dodged the flame, and threw himself against the door, meeting the force of her resistance. Enraged, she thrust the flame at him again and this time he felt the heat of it flap past his ear. And then he heard the heynim, a gigantic swarm swirling around her head, and trailing back into the dark beyond. He staggered out into the passage, clutching his ears. Caidrun watched him, the torch stuck out at arm's length to keep him at bay, then she reached once more to swing the door shut. Her face: so *white*! And her eyes, her clear blue eyes so dark and sunken in her face.

"Caidy, don't. I've come all the way from Minavar. Aren't you glad to see me?"

She paused, the door almost closed. "I hate you! How dare you come here now!" The door whoofed shut, cutting off her chimes. Tamborel stared at it blankly. *Move! Before she bolts it into place!* He leapt, seized the door ring, twisted it, and pushed. The door gave, and he slipped through. She was ready with the brand, but this time so was Tamborel. He seized it and held it out of reach. "Where have you been?"

She glared up at him, a gnarl of fury in her throat.

"I tried to find you, Caidy! I've been waiting for you all this time."

"Liar."

He looked around. "What is this place?"

"You'd be surprised." She looked sly now.

Tamborel eyed her closely. Whatever else she had become, she was no mist wraith. "How can you live down here? There's no air, no light. There's nothing to eat."

"Oh yes there is. And people."

Tamborel glanced into the darkness. More of Caidy's fancies? "Where?"

"Never you mind."

"Caidy, I heard chimes."

"Well, of course you did." She pointed to the swarm above her head.

"No, I heard more than that. Caidy, where—"

"Go away, *leave*!"

Tamborel shook his head. "When I've just found you?"

She threw herself on him, pushing him back. "Why now, why now! I hate you! You left me, you didn't care!"

"Not true!" Tamborel shouted. He went on, his voice lowered. "Caidy, I ran after you. All the way to Minavar. I even went to see Silwender. He told me to wait there, in the Hon'faleyn. He said you'd come, that anyone with your gift would end up there. So I waited, and waited, until things got so bad I came to find you."

"Bad?"

"Oh, Caidy, it was so hard to get here through the rains."

"Rains?" Caidrun sneered. "You think I don't keep tally down here? It's way past monsoon time."

Tamborel lifted the edge of his cloak. "Feel this. The monsoons are still raging and no signs of letting up."

Caidrun covered her ears. "Stop it. You lie."

"I never lie to you." Tamborel pressed on. "Hardly any heynim came last year, and none came this. Heynim are what hold this world together, don't you know? Now they're failing, the world's falling apart." He stepped forward, forcing her back now. "I suspected why, and now I know. The heynim are down here. You've snagged them and stowed them yonder. Oh, Caidy, how could you?" He moved to take her in his arms.

Caidrun started back, her swarm bouncing off the rocky walls. "Don't move another step!"

He stopped, reaching out his free hand. "Come to Minavar. Silwender can help you. We can both learn together."

"Learn?" Hope came to her eyes, softening her face. But then it was gone, and the old look was back. "Why now, after all this time?"

"I told you. Things are really bad up there. The crops failed last year. Now the rains won't end. People are hungry and sick. If this all doesn't stop soon, it will be worse than you could guess—for you and me and everyone. Caidy, let me help you put things right—please?"

She pointed to the outer door. "Go, now."

"We'll both go, after we've released the heynim." Tamborel pushed past her, holding the torch aloft. Shadows fled before him, over the rough stone floor. Then the far cave wall loomed, and in it, just as he'd suspected, a deeply recessed doorway.

"No!" Caidrun ran ahead to block him. "I shan't let you." As Tamborel reached the door and bent to raise the latch, Caidrun tried to fight him off. "You'll be sorry!" she warned, but Tamborel scarcely heard. As his fingers touched the latch, the shimmering that had guided him there rushed through him like the foamy rapids in the brook. He seized the latch and twisted it.

"*No!*" Caidrun beat him with her fists, but Tamborel only tightened his grip and pulled. Slowly, with a groaning sound, the massive door swung open.

Tamborel dropped the torch and fell against the door frame. Before him a solid mass of spheres crammed a space so vast he could not see the roof, could not guess how far back it stretched. Torches flickered from crevices in the walls to either side, the fitful flames reflected in the countless shiny spheres. And the noise! He looked at Caidrun in horror. "And you say you don't know what you've done?"

Caidrun looked triumphant. "It's quieter in Fahwyll now, I'll wager."

222

"*Fahwyll*!" Tamborel pushed away from the door. He pictured the lines of sick and hungry people, and Keiryn waiting with an old man who might be dead by now. "You fool, Caidy! When did you last climb those steps?"

"Don't call me a fool. I haven't, and I won't."

He seized her arm and shook her roughly. "Listen! The world is *dying*. Not even the Sky Spinners can stop it—and you give me drivel about Fahwyll!" He felt his anger rise, strove to control it. That would only make things worse. He took a breath, tried again. "For the past year or so I've scarcely slept from worrying about you. I've had the worst nightmares."

"Poor Brel." Caidrun's mouth curled. "You made your choice."

"Yes, I did. As I said, I followed you the very night you left, but you gave me no chance to find you. Caidy—trust me: the world is ending. Set the heynim loose."

"It won't work, Brel. You're trying to make me feel bad, the way the others used to. I'm not the fool you just called me."

Tamborel looked down on her tight, set face, at his wit's end now. "Of course not. And I'm for you, whatever you've done. Caidy, you can still put things right."

"Hah!"

"Do you want the world to die?"

"Don't be so dramatic, Brel."

Dramatic! "I'll make you see." He seized her arm and, taking up the fallen torch, began to drag her to the outer door. Caidrun fought to pull away until, halfway there, she lashed out with her foot, nicking his shin.

"Oh, you—" Tamborel turned on her, wincing in pain, but Caidrun danced out of reach, taunting him as of old. "Poor Brel. Did it hurt? Poor Brel, Brel the Heynless. Brel—go home!"

He straightened, looking at her sadly. "What you did was foolish, Caidy. You didn't know any better. But what you do now is *evil*."

He heard the hiss of her breath as she drew herself up. "Evil? I'll show you evil. Here:" The pent-up spheres behind her began to move.

"No!" he shouted, but the heynim burst through the door and streamed toward him, gathering speed.

·25·

The shining pellets converged upon him, hiding Caidy from view. Casting the torch aside, Tamborel raised his arms to cover his face. All at once, the heynim checked, lurched, then came on again. He heard Caidy's scream.

"Brel—I cannot stop them!"

She burst through the heyn-mass, hurling herself upon him. As their bodies collided, he threw out his arms, and down they went. His whole being recoiled from remembered pain. But this time, a part of him said, they'd strike Caidy, piercing her to the bone. "No! No! No!" It began as a shout, ended as a roar. With an almighty effort, he pushed her aside and knelt up, eyes closed, bending his mind to the on-coming fury. Time stretched. Then, in the space of an instant, the wall of sound rolled on toward him like a wave bursting its river banks at full spring flood. He braced, pushed his will against it, recoiled in shock. Another second, and the spheres would hit!

Back! Back!

Over the tumult came a hum. The humming rose to a whine like that of a twister advancing across the open fields. Even as he strained, he covered his ears, grimacing with pain. Caidrun cried out, then all went dark.

Tamborel lay on his back, gazing up at deep blue sky. Beside him, heynim jingled musically. Water rushed nearby. Someone stroked his head. "Brel. Brel, I'm sorry. . . ."

He opened his eyes. Caidy bent over him. The blue sky was gone, and the sound of the brook. All was dark, save for flickering firelight. He was lying on rock floor, his head in Caidrun's lap. Above and be-yond, the dim space was alive with spheres, the van-guard of the masses still jamming the inner cavern.

"I thought you were dead." A tear splashed onto his face.

He struggled up, put his arms around her. "I'm fine, Caidy." It was all coming back now. The con-verging heynim. Caidy's shout.

"*Brel—I cannot stop them!*" If she had not halted their rush, then who? He looked up at the seething canopy of spheres.

She put her arms around him and squeezed. "You did it, Brel. You made a sort of . . . soundstorm. It was terrifying. Then you fell even though they didn't touch you and I thought—" She dug her face into his chest.

Tamborel stared up, surveying the shifting golden canopy. *He* had done that? He remembered now how she'd thrown herself upon him, recalled his terror as the spheres had shot toward them, the thought that Caidy would be hurt. He slid an arm about her shoulders. How light they felt, and fragile. What she needed was fresh air and sunshine, and good, solid food. He let out a quiet sigh that was quite lost in the chiming. Sitting there on that deep cold floor he felt content as he'd not felt since they'd left Fahwyll.

Complete.

Suddenly, he laughed. Caidy looked up, wary. "What, Brel?"

"Two halves, together again at last." He brushed his hand lightly over her tangled, wiry hair. More like frytt-burrs than ever, he thought.

She pulled away. "You snagged the heynim. You can hold on your own now. You don't need me any more."

He grinned down at her. "You think that's it? You have no idea. We're going to have so much fun, you and I. Wait till we get back to Minavar. You have so many new friends to meet: Keiryn, and Jareyd, Hewl, and Synla. They're going to love you, Caidy, just see."

"You think so?"

"Bet on it!"

Caidrun leaned back against him, reassured. Tamborel let out a long slow breath, savoring the moment. Just as he'd pictured it, finally. Above them, the heynim jostled and collided, setting up delicate, random harmonies. Tamborel gazed up, thinking. What he'd just done: could he do it again? He nodded the nearest intyl to him. It came! "Caidy, look!"

Caidrun smiled. She let go, and shifted around, nestling into him. "Again, Brel. Again."

Tamborel snagged a second intyl, then a third. Now he pulled in a scattering of anintyl, then a fistful of omantyl. Caidy's voice came, very low he could scarcely hear. "Music, Brel. Make music."

His breath caught in his throat. *Oosiks, Brel. Oosiks.* He closed his eyes, feeling Caidy's warmth against him, and began to tune to the ancient fire of Caidrun's deep, abiding wrath, threw on it the salt of bitterness. Sound sparks flew, the faleyn exploded, bursting against the cavern walls, echoing off the vaulted roof. The chimes swelled, the noise was deafening. White wrath-fire flashed in the darkness, then faded to a dull red ache, and died to pale gray ashes, vanishing. In the lull, Tamborel spun a quiet skein of melancholy. Of Caidrun's hopelessness, of his own days and nights of sadness and loss. The chimes drifted like a veil around the cavern. At last, he let the muted harmonies fade. Now the heyn-mass melted into randomness, quiet mourners milling after a wake.

For a while they sat, then Caidy looked up. "Oh, Brel. It was so *bad.*"

"But it's all gone now." He took her hand and pulled them upright.

"Come on."

"Tamborel, I daren't."

He put his arm around her. "It's all right. You'll be fine."

"I've done a wicked thing."

"Silwender will understand."

They started toward the outer door. "Wait. I have to say good-bye."

"You mean—there really are folk down here?"

"Oh, yes. They think I'm one of them, though funny in the head, because I'm so different."

So: she'd been an outcast down here, too. . . .

"They don't know of the stair?"

"No. And I didn't tell them."

"Do they know about the heynim?"

"Yes, though not what I did with them." She looked up at him earnestly. "Those people *make* them, Brel."

"Make them!" So, he thought. Caidy had been right. And without benefit of book or teacher had traced them to their source. "How?"

"I can't say exactly. I've seen some of what they do—though I've never seen the mines. They lie really deep. But I've been to the caves where they smelt the ore, and shape the spheres. The most wonderful time is when they wheel the heynim in baskets to a huge cavern and have a sort of Gathering. It's to release the heynim up a round hole like a chimney in the cavern roof.

"When I learned about the Gathering, I found a gap in the chimney wall, at this level we're on now. I blocked the chimney just above the gap. As the heynim floated up, I drew them out and hid them here."

"The chimney's still blocked?"

Caidrun nodded.

"Then we must clear it before we do anything else."

They took up torches and set off, the heynim trailing like a golden river. Presently, Tamborel felt a draft. Rock wall loomed across their path.

"The chimney wall?"

Caidrun nodded. "See the gap?" A ragged breach in the stone about waist height. Handing Caidrun his torch, Tamborel leaned into the gap. Just above his head was a solid plug of stones, tightly jammed together. He reached up, gripped a wedge of stone, and pulled, starting a small avalanche. Way below, there came faint echoes of rock striking rock.

The echoes died. The rock had finished falling. Tamborel poked his head cautiously through the gap. Way above, a speck of dull gray light. He ducked his head out again and stepped back, blinking mist droplets from his eyes. Now to release the heynim. "Ready, Caidy?"

"Oh, yes!"

Tamborel took her hands. *Two years' worth of heynim*: never again in his lifetime—in anybody's! He'd already tuned *some* of it to Caidy's healing. And now? "Caidy, close your eyes."

"What—"

"Hush."

Caidrun obeyed.

As the heynim stream flowed past toward the chimney hole, he looped it spirally around them, until they stood inside a chiming, golden pillar. A small whirlwind sprang up about them, lifting their hair. At its touch, Caidrun's hands tightened in his, but beyond that, she did not stir.

Closing his own eyes now, Tamborel bent his full power to the swarm, pouring out all the wishes and hopes that he'd kept in his heart for Caidrun since the beginning. The tunnel walls resounded with brilliant, joyous chiming as the heynim swirled around them then streamed on up toward the sky: a Grand Concatenation carrying all the way to Minavar!

Long after the last heyn had passed, they stood locked together in the spell of those chimes. Way above, wind soughed in the hollow chimney. Presently, Caidrun sighed and stirred against him.

"How quiet it is," he murmured. Eerie, with all the chimes gone. Yet he didn't feel unease. He pictured the seemingly endless swarm racing down toward the plain. Keiryn catching the first faint notes and running out to witness that wondrous swarm sweep eastward. Keiryn. Then the outermost settlers. Then Minavar. Tamborel smiled up into the darkness. The whole world caught up in a song of love as could never come again.

"I'd better go," Caidy said, then, all at once, she began to laugh.

"What is it?"

She pointed to the empty space above his head. "Brel the Heynless!" Then she pointed at herself. "Caidrun the Heynless, too. I let mine go with the others. I'll have to start from scratch, along with you. Here: this can be your very first one." She pulled an intyl from a pocket and held it up with finger and thumb. "Silwender's," she said, nodding it toward him. "I stowed it so I wouldn't lose it in the mass."

"Caidy, I can't."

"Please."

The little thing bobbed and dipped around his head, its familiar tones tinkling good as new. "Thanks."

"Now," Caidrun went on briskly. "I have to go and take my leave. I'll tell them about the stairway now, though they likely won't believe me."

Tamborel thought of those deep folk, and wondered. Who they were, how they had come to be down there, how they had forgotten about the stair. He grew curious. "Shall I go with you?"

"I'd rather do it alone, if you don't mind." She looked away. Saying good-bye was not going to be wholly easy, Tamborel thought. Even if they had thought her strange, someone had been kind, had fed and clothed her. And she wanted to keep it private, for now.

"Very well. I'll wait for you up here. Maybe it's best to leave them to Silwender, anyway." News of these folk would rock the Hon'faleyn to its foundations, he thought, as Caidrun took his hand, towing him along. "You won't be too long, will you?"

"Oh, no." She gave his hand a little squeeze. "Only a few hours ago, I was so full of hate, Brel. I wanted everyone to suffer as much as I did. But now I want to get up there and see some sun."

"By the time we get up those steps, you just may get your wish, Caidy."

They reached the tunnel that led down to the lower levels. "You keep the torch. I don't need one. You'll be all right?"

Tamborel nodded. Oh, yes, he'd be all right, now. He leaned against the tunnel wall, savoring the unaccustomed jingle of the single intyl just above his head. Silwender's gift to Caidy. Her gift to him. Not a swarm, exactly. But a good beginning. . . .

Pronunciation Guide

PROPER NAMES:

Alyafaleyn	Alley-*a*'fa-lain (*a*'s as in *cat*)
Caidrun	*Kay*'drun (*u* as in *put*)
Casinder	Kas-*in*'duh (*a* as in *cat*)
Cerie	*Seer*'y
Eleyna	Ell-*lain*'uh
Fahwyll	*Fah*'wyll
Hwyllum	*Hwyll*'um (sound `h'; *u* as in *put*)
Meynoc	*May*'nock
Pridicum	*Prid*'ick-um (*i*'s as in *pin*; *u* as in *put*)
Rufina	Roo-*feen*'uh
Silwender	Sill-*wend*'uh
Tamborel	*Tam*'bor-ell
Tam'shu	*Tam*'shoo
Yornwey	*Yawn*'way

COMMON NOUNS:

faleyn	*fa*'lain (*a* as in *cat*)
heyn	hain
intyl	*in*'till
omantyl	oh-*mahn*'till
qarl	kahl
saba	*sah*'buh
saraba	sa-*rah*'buh
zjarn	sahn (*s* as in *measure*)

234